MW00460744

ANT

ANT

Collected short stories, war serials and
selected poems of C.K. Scott Moncrieff

Edited by Jean Findlay

SCOTLAND STREET PRESS

Copyright © 2015 Jean Findlay
All rights reserved.

Scotland Street Press
7/1 Scotland Street
Edinburgh EH3 6PP

ISBN: 978-1-910895-00-9

Typeset in Dante MT by Palimpsest Book Production Limited,
Falkirk, Stirlingshire

Printed in Scotland by Bell & Bain Limited, Glasgow

Jacket design based on a 1940's edition of *Remembrance of Things Past*
by Marcel Proust, translated by C K Scott Moncrieff,
published by Chatto and Windus.

To a Friend Without a Name.

Through lazy summer afternoons
I wreathed slow thoughts to unsung tunes.
And you some winter evening may
Take up my finished book and say
"This molten thought was his- who wrought
No less the thoughts of elder men–"
Or, closing, curse too feeble verse,
The penned, the penman, and the pen.

No matter what you think or do
This book is yours and made for you
Take it and read it through

CKSM 1906

Contents

Introduction

Charles Kenneth Scott Moncrieff, who lived from 1889 to 1930, is known for his masterly translation of Proust's *Remembrance of Things Past*. Both Joseph Conrad and Scott Fitzgerald thought his translation better than Proust's novel itself. He could not, however, have been such a great translator had he not been an imaginative and experimental writer himself, trying all forms of poetry at a young age, publishing short stories and, unique at that time, a weekly serial on the life of a soldier in the trenches.

Competent translation requires knowledge of the language, good translation involves that and knowledge of the era as well as experience of the social milieu of the writer; great translation demands flexibility, an imaginative gift, the speed of instinct – "the flash of one poet catching almost intuitively the emotion of another long dead" as the *Times Literary Supplement* wrote of Scott Moncrieff's rendering of the *Chanson de Roland* in 1919. Nearly a hundred years later in 2014, A.N Wilson in the same periodical wrote; "Scott Moncrieff is more Proustian than Proust himself."

He lived through the same era as Proust and experienced the neuroticism of fin de siècle decadence as well as the tough self-knowledge that came with fighting in the war. Certainly he felt the terrors and pitfalls of being, like Proust, a closeted homosexual, and he expressed it from an early age. *Evensonge and Morwesong* is a short story written when Charles was eighteen and published in the *New Field*, the school magazine which he edited. The magazine was instantly withdrawn and pulped and Charles was prevented from going to Oxford.

The title is taken from the *Prologue* of Chaucer's *Canterbury Tales* "If evensong and morwesong accorde, let's see who shall tell the first tale . . ." It is a tale of the loss of innocence, of a sexual act committed between schoolboys. It satirizes a master of a public school who is about to punish a boy for a similar offence when the remembers he was guilty of this himself at school. For some reason this makes him harsher, blinder and more punitive: the guilt gives him a black energy. The story is about snobbery, hypocrisy and school masters. It has a precocious psychological and emotional insight and was a courageous tale to tell in 1908.

Scott Moncrieff went on to become a soldier in WW1 and was decorated for bravery. The War infused the rest of his stories. These were published by G K Chesterton in the *New Witness*, by T S Eliot in the *New Criterion* and by J C Squire in the *London Mercury*. *Mortmain* is a ghost story about a wounding, where the amputated limb has a life of its own. All these stories witness the great social changes that took place after the First World War. The very idea that servants were equal as human beings, not a sort of sub species, was radical in the upper classes and two stories: *The Victorians* and *Cousin Fanny and Cousin Annie* illustrate this social chasm and its heartbreaking consequences. *Cousin Fanny and Cousin Annie* is also experimentally Proustian; involving tangential childhood memories and the strong bond between a child and the household cook, like Marcel and Francoise in *Swann's Way*. However the ending is spare and rough, more Dostoevsky than Proust. The soldier narrator enters the bare, single room, "frowsty with the smell of poverty" to discover Annie the cook has died the evening before.

> He had stood this way by many of his intimate friends during the last five years, had lain awake in hospital wards where someone or other died every night, had helped bury brother officers, and men of his own company, when the ground was

frozen too hard for a pick to break it; but Annie dead; Annie to whom he had scarcely given a thought all that time, was different. He knelt by the bed, sobbing, felt for her hard little hand and kissed it again and again, then rose and stooped over her face and kissed her shining forehead . . .

He recalled for the first time all the "laborious, loving , ungrudging service of all those years, poured out for himself and other people without any question of their response to her."

There are two Saki-esque satires namely *The Mouse in the Dovecote* and *Two Tales*. Interestingly Saki and Scott Moncrieff shared the same country house hostess – Saki pre-war and Scott Moncrieff post-war. *Ant* satirizes the small, small life of upper class Britain and the society that Scott Moncrieff was tired of by the time he left to live in Italy.

The War Serial, beginning with *Halloween*, was a weekly story for the *New Witness* and he wrote it while in the trenches and on sick leave with trench foot in 1916. It is raw experience translated to the page – it conveys not unmitigated horror but a soldier's day to day life at the front in all its aspects: camaraderie, humour, surprise, shock and the ghastly stiffs, waxen in the moonlight on Halloween. We learn the practicalities of being in charge of a hungry Company of men and finding food while on the move; killing farm animals, milking a stray goat, bartering for bread, and finding somewhere, anywhere dry, to sleep. Allison is the main character in all of these episodes , and Scott Moncrieff admits that Allison is someone "with whose identity the present writer has become totally bound up".

Field Discipline addresses the problem of military court martials and their outcome; they were not all blindly punitive, many succeeded in freeing the soldier in the dock, even when 'guilty'.

The Poems are divided in to Early Poems written from the age of 15, and are mixed in quality; some erotic and dedicated to friends and some showing an advanced spiritual understanding. The War poems start with *Billets* – a set of verses which can be seen as an extension of Charles the officer constantly trying to jolly along his men. The poems become serious and later critical and one despondent. Many again show his awareness of the 'other side', how this earthly battle is mirrored by the battle for each man's soul, in particular the poem written at the time of his wounding, *The Face of Raphael*. Another war poem, *Summer Thunder*, is a vision of ancient warriors living in underground caverns reminiscent of Tolkein, and takes a theme Scott Moncrieff likes, that of finding empathy with all soldiers throughout the ages.

Among the Love poems are several written to Wilfred Owen, with whom Scott Moncrieff fell in love in 1918. Also dedications to other friends, lost in the war; these are moving and poignant. The Satirical Verses are cryptic and require a knowledge of political events of the time to understand . I make no apologies for including them, placing them at the end of the collection, as wit and satire are very much part of the picture of the man as a whole.

I hope this collection completes the complex portrait of the man laid out in the biography *Chasing Lost Time*, and will allow the reader the chance to hear Charles Scott Moncrieff's own idiosyncratic literary voice.

Jean Findlay
Edinburgh 2015

SHORT STORIES

EVENSONGE AND MORWESONG

I.

. . . "And if we are found out?" asked Maurice. He was still on his knees in the thicket, and, as he looked up to where his companion stood in an awkward fumbling attitude, his face seemed even more than unusually pale and meagre in the grey broken light. It was with rather forced nonchalance that Carruthers answered "O, the sack, I suppose" – and he stopped aghast at the other's expression. Then as only at one other time in a long and well-rewarded life did he feel that a millstone around his neck might perhaps be less offensive than the picture of those small, startled features hung for all eternity before his eyes.

But all went well. Each returned to his house (they were at school at Gainsborough – this in the early eighties) without let or hindrance. When in the next autumn but one Carruthers went up to Oxford I doubt if he remembered his debt to the Creator of the soul of Edward Hilary Maurice. "After all, had he been so scrupulous?" he argued, "I am no worse than a dozen others and Maurice no better. Indeed Maurice is getting quite a reputation. How dreadful all that sort of thing is!" And what ever he may have remembered at Oxford, we may be certain that when with his charming nonchalance he knelt before a golfer-bishop of no mean hysterical attractions to receive deacon's orders, he presented himself as a pure, sincere, and fragrant vessel, capable of containing any amount of truth.

II.

William Carruthers turned a trifle uneasily in his stiff, new revolving chair as his victims entered. It was the last day of October. For a little more than a month he had occupied the headmaster's study at Cheddar, a school for which as a pious Gainsburgher he retained a profound contempt. This contempt was hardly diminished (to do him justice his salary was but moderate) by his having already to deal with one of those painful incidents which occur in second-rate schools almost as frequently as in the sacred Nine.

What he said to them is not our province. His weighty arguments (mainly borrowed from the boys' housemaster), his ears deaf to excuse or contradiction, his flaying sarcasm and his pessimistic prophecies drew great salt tears from the younger boy's eyes on to the gaudy new magisterial carpet before that unfortunate was sent away heavily warned against further out-breaks, and he was left free to damn the other in this world and disparage him in the next. He eyed him witheringly for some minutes, and then whispered: "Ah, Hilary! It were better for thee that a millstone were hanged about thy neck , and thou cast into the sea, than that thou shouldst offend one of these little ones." He had previously consulted a concordance, and in variously impressive tones rehearsed this and the parallel passages. Chance or inspiration might have prompted Hilary, whose whole life was being ruined to correct his first offence, to cite the following verses (read in Chapel an evening or two before) which enjoin that seven offences on the same day should be balanced by the offender's penitence. But he was silent. Carruthers, supposing him unrepentant and inveterate, lathed him with abuse that ranged from ribaldry to a little less than rhetoric; and finally dismissed him to remove his effects from his house and from Cheddar, whither he might, if well behaved, return in ten years' time.

These effectual workings over, the headmaster turned to the second part of the expulsion office – the letter to parent or guardian. It was then that he remembered his ignorance of the boy's address, and with some repugnance turned to a gaudy volume inscribed *Ordo Cheddarensis* in gold upon a red, blue and green back and sides, which had appeared there synchronically with himself. In the index he was faintly surprised to find: "Hilary, see Maurice, J. E.H."; and he was annoyed at the consequent delay. At last he found the reference, laid down the book (which crackled cheerily in its stiff, cheap binding), and read up his man:

"Maurice, James Edward Hilary (now J. E. H. Hilary). Born 13 Sept., 18—. Only son of Edward Hilary Maurice (now E. H. Hilary), of Leaflseigh, Co. Southampton, who on succeeding to that estate assumed the name of Hilary in lieu of that of Maurice. Adresses: 13 Worcester Gate Terrace, W.; Leaflseigh, Christchurch Road, R. S. O., Hants."

As he was transcribing the address this most consummate of headmasters received an unpleasant shock. Its pages released, the book crackled inexpensively and closed itself. In its place lay or floated a picture of two boys in a thicket; of the one's charming nonchalance; of terror sickening the other, a child that had just lost its soul. When at Oxford Carruthers had received a letter in which Maurice said: "It is not altogether because I must leave Gainsborough that I curse you now. But I can never send my sons there, nor to any decent school. Shorncliffe must receive them, or Milkmanthaite or even Cheddar – some hole that we have thought hardly worth our scorn. Because my sons will inherit the shame which you implanted, I now for the last time call you . . . . . ." Carruthers' fine British reserve had elided the next words from his memory.

Before his ordination he had prayed for spiritual armour, and had received a coat of self-satisfaction which had so far held out against all assaults of man or woman. Now it felt rusty. Rather half-heartedly he rang and told the butler to send someone to Mr Herbertson's house to tell Mr Hilary that the headmaster wanted him again and at once. Then he picked up the sheet of tremendously coat-armoured school notepaper, upon which a laboured and almost illegible "My dear Sir" was begun. On it he drew obscene figures for half-an-hour. Then the messenger returned. "Please sir", reported the butler, "James that I sent up, sir, says he couldn't find no one in Mr Herbertson's house for him to speak to, leastways but Mrs Wrenn, the housekeeper. She said, sir, as how Mr Hilary had just gone off to the station in a fly with all of his luggage."

The headmaster of Cheddar took up his mortarboard and went out, swearing indiscriminately.

This was written in 1907 when CKSM was 18 and published in the New Field. Later published in 1923 by Francis Murray in a limited edition.

MORTMAIN

"Oh, so easy — enn, enn, enn, — easy — enn, enn, enn, enn, — EASY — enn, enn, enn, — enn, enn, — easy — enn — enn — e-n-n — e-a-s-y."

Impotent to control or to resist his movements, Farleigh Bennet had been carried into and laid down in a small hut that served as an ante-room to the theatre proper. A friendly stranger, whom he had seen from the ground imperfectly, standing somewhere beyond the roof of his head, had thereupon taken charge of him, and, bidding him place his sound arm so and lie quite easy, had placed over his mouth and nostrils the mask through which the maddening sweet drug percolated. For a time, the anaesthetist's last word 'easy' lingered in his ears; then a succession of small, four-pointed silver stars shot into his skull, fell through his brain like gravel into a pond, and settled in a linoleum pattern on the dark green floor of his consciousness. They stung him oddly in their falling, yet fell, irresistible, more and more. No words sounded now in his ears, and, struggling more and more feebly to resist the stinging freezing stars, consciousness dwindled and went out of him.

In the theatre, meanwhile, a surgeon examined the imported body with a professional interest dulled by his long day's work there, but with a human sympathy which the odd circumstances, so far as they had reached him, of the casualty considerably quickened; Bennet had not been wounded in any glorious encounter; a bomb badly thrown by a man of his own Company had fallen back at his feet from the parapet and, while he groped for it in the dark trench, had exploded actually under his right hand. These three extremities were so shattered as to make amputation the one possible remedy; the operations were quickly performed, without difficulty, and Farleigh Bennet, bandaged and blanketed, was replaced on his stretcher and carried back to his bed in the long marquee – three marquees joined in one, rather – which composed a ward of a General Hospital on the coast of the Pas de Calais.

He had gone after nine to the theatre, and at midnight he was still regaining consciousness. At first the long tent seemed to him an occupied trench, lighted – by some unexplained new convention – with electricity. He had men there, he felt drowsily, under him, and in his mind imagined journeys to right and left of him, of inspection and command. Then he knew himself to be actually in bed, and remembered the reason. But with the act of memory his mutilated legs and arm assumed personalities outside his own, and strongly discordant from one another. Once again he was in command, but only of his own members – and his command one scattered and undisciplined. But not so scattered, for his legs assumed now the air of two women jostling one another on the steps of the omnibus. Swaddled in gauze and cotton-wool, they both felt stout and seemed to carry parcels. His arm kept sullenly aloof: why – he remembered his bed again – should all these be herded together? Physically separate, there should be a bed for each one of them . . .. The bed passed from his consciousness: he tasted the heavy air of the tent and knew himself on the bare plateau behind Carnoy. He had men under him, a carrying party, but they were scattered in single file through the darkness. Those two lights; one of them must be at the dump where he was to call for stores: but which? He had lost his direction and must go to each light in turn: they were so far off, though, that he would never reach either. Besides, he could not move out of bed. It was all suddenly clear again. His limbs were in one bed with him because, though the place was full of beds, all the beds were full. It was a place for suffering mortality. He recognized in the lights now two electric globes. They had been turned on when the night-sister came, before he went to the theatre. He had halted for a moment under one, opposite the screened bed where an Australian Colonel was dying. Had been dying, rather, it was so many hours ago: could anyone still be alive? Bennet turned his head, trying to catch sight of the screens, but they were beyond his small range of vision. There was a tent-pole not far from him, which creaked just audibly at short irregular intervals. Against the pole leaned a somnolent orderly, a large Union Jack folded over his arm. So the Colonel was gone at last; for that flag meant death. He had just died and they were giving him a few minutes to settle down in the next world, before carrying out his body. Its outline would be hardly discernable between the flag and the stretcher: men got so thin then. Someone else would have the bed to-morrow. It must be very easy to die. Hundreds of people died in these hospitals, almost unnoticed.

Suddenly he jerked his arm in its wooden framework – and with that pain lost consciousness of the ward and saw only darkness. His wrist felt hot suddenly, but his ankles were still very cold. Two lights shone out and became steady. He knew himself now to be in one of the darkened streets of London – Shaftesbury Avenue. The doors of a theatre were opposite, and, as he watched them, the audience began to come out. There were no cabs passing, but it was a dry evening; very, parchingly dry. People scattered in front of him, their faces obscure and unimportant. But, as the theatre emptied, he could see his wife's face distinctly. She had worn that cloak last time he was on leave; open at the neck shewing her pearls. That was risky, in the street. They had seen several plays together then; surely they must have been to some theatre to-night. Yes; of course he had been. But his legs and arms jostled him so, that he could not get at her. Beyond, he made out a man's figure: that poisonous ass Courtly Smith came up behind her, talking over her shoulder. He had implored her not to go about with the man. He must tell her again, now; decisively, this time; and, trying to sit up and call her, found his mouth and nostrils filled again with the savour of chloroform – and sank back on his pillows unconscious.

II.

Claire Bennet unlocked the door of her flat, leaving it ajar behind her, as Courtly Smith would come up when he had paid off the cabman.

On the hall table lay a telegram which she took up and carelessly opened. "O.H.M.S", she read, "Captain F. Bennet admitted to Hospital 8th instant. Severe gun-shot wounds right arm and both legs a-a-a Present location unknown a-a-a Presumably your husband." Poor Farleigh: severely wounded. Perhaps Courtly Smith had better not come in to-night. The maid would chatter if she heard him. Claire walked out to the landing and leaned over the well of the stair. She could see or hear nothing, and went back into the drawing-room, closing the outer-door gently. The fire was still burning behind a wire screen which chequered the room with its shadow: she turned on a reading lamp by the piano, and moved it to the mantel-piece. As she raised it, the cord seemed to be caught, and held by something, and the lamp was almost pulled from her hand. A quiet knocking sounded from the front door: as she left the room again, the lamp was suddenly extinguished.

When she unlatched the door, Courtly Smith pushed it gently open and stood for a moment on the mat, looking into her face.

"I think you had better not come in to-night." she whispered, shivering a little in the draught from the stair.

"Tired, dear?" he asked carelessly.

"Yes; rather." She half turned, looking into the darkness of the drawing-room. "Go in. The lamp is on the mantel-piece."

As he crossed the hall, she saw beyond him the wire screen move diagonally forwards from the fender, and its network of shadows creep across the dimly-lit floor.

She stood on the threshold of the room as he groped across the mantel-piece for the lamp. He had taken it in his left hand when she saw him fling his head violently backwards. While she felt for the main switch inside the door, he made with the lamp a sweeping stroke through the air between his face and the fireplace. It crashed into the fender, and, as she filled the room with light from ceiling cluster he staggered backwards and fell upon the sofa, plucking heavily with both hands at his throat. She went nearer; a foot trod heavily upon hers; through her thin stocking she felt the cold pressure of an invisible heel. Looking at him for an explanation she caught only the agony in his eyes; the look of a man in deadly and incomprehensible pain. A foot was pressed against her left leg, above the knee; she could feel the pressure of each toe, driving the small beads of her frock into the skin. She looked up again; he lay back on the sofa, his hands still tearing at his throat, his legs writhing convulsively.

The maid had good cause to chatter from the moment when, going in with a cup of tea for her mistress, she found the bedroom empty. In the drawing room, a dead man was sprawling across the sofa. The ceiling lights still burned but the curtains were parted. Outside on the balcony, Claire sat, laughing unevenly. The string of her necklace had broken, and upon her lap was a little pool of pearls, one of which, from time to time, she flung to the sparrows, splashing, quarrelling and courting in the dust of the courtyard.

III.

In the dimly lighted tent the night sister saw no more, when she went off duty, than that Farleigh Bennet seemed to be quietly sleeping after the operation. But a day-nurse, who had come to wash him, called shrilly for an orderly, screens were brought. Breakfast was a little delayed in the ward and a young officer at the far end turned for solace to the gramophone, of which he had tacitly become controller. His new records had not arrived from England, and most of the rest he and the other patients had broken when petulance overcame mere boredom. So that it was from a limited choice rather than with any conscious attempt at irony that, after winding up the machine he lowered its needle on to the disc labelled "Who were you with last night?"

Published in The New Witness, edited by GK Chesterton
December 8, 1922

COUSIN FANNY AND COUSIN ANNIE

I.

The house seemed very big, that first day, to Alec; he was so little, and it was so dark and full of wonderful things, with doors every-where behind which there must be more wonderful things still hidden. And it was quite a long way across the drawing-room to the chair in which Cousin Fanny was sitting, so that she had time to make her face smile before he reached her. Alec could make his face smile, too, in the big mirror with legs in his mother's room, but his smiled more quickly than Cousin Fanny's, and by the time she had stroked his head and asked him how his father was her face was quite sad again, and he thought that she must be sad because his father and mother were going back to India, and he loved Cousin Fanny for being sad, but her sadness made him so sad that he almost began to cry. Then Cousin Fanny seemed frightened, and felt in a crumpled little paper bag on the table beside her until she found a lozenge like a blackberry which she told him to put in his mouth and suck carefully; and while he was sucking it carefully she said, with a little noise in her throat which made him want to laugh: "Run away now and see if Annie had something nice for you". And Alec's mother, who had been standing behind him, took him out of the room and downstairs and through one of the doors into another room which was quite small and very hot, and full of gold and silver things, dish-covers and pots and pans, and a little person in a very dirty dress ran to meet him and caught him under the arms and put him standing on the table, and walked all round and clucked her tongue at him and said "Well, well". And this was Annie. And Alec's mother left him there and went back to talk to Cousin Fanny, and before he got down from the table Annie told him that his father had stood on the same table when he was no bigger than Alec, "and now he can eat the grass off the top of my head", she said; and that was so funny, Alec laughed and looked at the top of her head to see if there was really any grass on it. And then he kissed her on her forehead, which was very shiny because she had to stand all day before the hot fire, and she lifted him down from the table and brought out a little mug with a picture of a hen and two chickens on it, and gave him his tea (which was only milk really, with a lump of sugar to sweeten it) and a little cake which she had baked for him, with ten currants on the top making a big A. And Alec said: "I can eat currants off the top of my cake!" and Annie laughed. And she told him the names of all the pots and pans, and showed him what was in each of the boxes, with pictures on the sides, and the box with the Queen's picture had tea in it, and the box with the picture of a poor Indian standing in a paddy-field had rice; and that made Alec sad because his father and mother were going to India next day. And then there was a noise in the corner, and a big hairy beast came and put his face on the table beside Alec and glared at him with eyes that were bright green like glass marbles; and Alec was frightened, but Annie said that it was only Cousin Fanny's dog, Gelert, and that he was very gentle. So Alec made friends with Gelert, and Gelert was very gentle with him, though Alec never like the smell Gelert made when he breathed in Alec's face. But Gelert knew not to lick Alec's face, and Alec liked him for that.

And after Annie had told him the name of everything in the kitchen, and Elizabeth, the maid, had come in and talked to them for a little, and they had showed him the photograph of poor Margaret, who had been the maid before Elizabeth, and had been found lying in a pool of blood, his mother took him away, and he said good-night to Cousin Fanny and his mother put him in a big iron bed in the room which was to be his very own; and when he was saying his prayers and had asked God to bless all the people he knew, his mother reminded him: "And Cousin Fanny", and Alec repeated, "And Cousin Fanny"; and then he went on "and Cousin

Annie, and make me good 'n 'beadjent for Jesus Christ's sake, amen". And his mother must have told Cousin Fanny when she went downstairs again, because next day, when his mother had gone to India, and he and Cousin Fanny were both feeling very sad, she smiled at him quite suddenly and said: "So you've found another cousin, Alec?" and Alec didn't know what she meant until she went on: "Annie's your cousin now, too, I hear". She spoke in such a queer voice that Alec thought she was angry, but he soon found out that she had a great many voices, and it depended on what she was saying which she used; and she was very often sad, but never angry.

II.

Cousin Annie told Alec that Cousin Fanny was sad not because his parents had gone to India, but because it was October. Her mother's birthday had been in October, and she was always sad then, but she was sadder still in May because that had been when her mother had died. Alec remembered May because the Queen's birthday was the twenty-fourth of then, and his mother had taken him to the barracks to see the Regiment on parade, and his father was riding on a horse; and Cousin Annie told him that it was on the Queen's birthday that Cousin Fanny's mother had died, and he was never to say anything about the Queen's birthday to Cousin Fanny. So Alec said that he had never been told about Cousin Fanny's mother dying then, and Cousin Annie explained that it had been a great many years ago, before Alec was born, and when his father had been quite a little boy. And Alec wondered, because his birthday was in October too, and he thought that he might have to die on the Queen's Birthday, when his father was riding on a horse in India. And when his birthday came he did not tell Cousin Fanny, because it was still October, but Cousin Fanny knew about his birthday and gave him a lovely present, and did not look sad all day. And when he was just going to bed he said: "Thank you very much for my nice birthday, and my lovely present, but I didn't want you to know". And she said, "Know what, dear?" And Alec had to explain: "About my birthday, because it's October". And Cousin Annie looked frightened for a moment, and then she took him in her arms and kissed him a great many times, and said he was a dear boy, and they both cried a little because it was so sad about Cousin Fanny's mother being dead. But he didn't like to ask Cousin Fanny if she thought that he would have to die too on the Queen's Birthday because he had been born in October.

III.

After Christmas, Alec began to do lessons at the house next door with the Watsons. Mrs Watson had a great many children, and two of the girls were younger than Alec, and George was a little older but not so big. Mr Watson was dead, too, but Mrs Watson didn't seem at all sad, and Alec thought she was like the old woman who lived in a shoe; she had so many children and she didn't know what to do. Their governess was called Miss Spearman, and she used to teach them lessons all morning, and then they had a schoolroom dinner together, and she took them for a walk in the afternoon. But presently Miss Spearman went away, and another governess came who was prettier and not so old, and made the children laugh at their lessons and they forgot about Miss Spearman.

Alec used to have his breakfast with Cousin Fanny before he went to his lessons, and after breakfast Cousin Fanny told him to ring the bell, and Annie came in with a Bible and a Book of Meditations, and Elizabeth put two chairs against the sideboard; and there was a hole in the sideboard between where the two chairs went, with a bowlful of water in case Gelert wanted a drink when he came into the dining-room, and there was a stick of sulphur in the water which was good for Gelert, Elizabeth said, and had always been there; and Cousin Fanny read Prayers. It was very dark in the winter mornings, and Cousin Fanny had to have the gas lighted, to see. And she read a chapter out of the Bible in a deep voice like a man's, and a Meditation for the Day in a very sad voice, and then she made a little noise in her throat, and the servants knelt down, and Alec was still too little, so he put his face on the table with his hands over his eyes, and Cousin Fanny said a long prayer, which Alec thought she made up out of her head, but Annie told him the prayers were all written down in a book that Cousin Fanny's mother used to have, long ago. And when she said the prayer her voice became very high and sweet, like the fifes at the barracks when they played Retreat, and sometimes the gas flickered and said 'peep' in a voice just like Cousin Fanny's, and Alec peeped through his fingers and saw Cousin Fanny's lips moving, and then he peeped at Annie and Elizabeth kneeling, and he thought how surprised God would be if He looked in at the window and saw their two backs leaning against the sideboard. And Alec laughed; but afterwards he said to Cousin Fanny that he was sorry he had laughed at Prayers, and he told her why, and Cousin Fanny said that nothing could surprise God.

On Sundays, Cousin Fanny took him with her to church, where the clergyman was a very good man all the same, but he had a rumbling voice and Alec could not understand what he said. But when the hymns came everybody else stood up and sang, and Cousin Fanny sang in a very sweet and sad voice, and there was a noise in the organ which had a voice just like Cousin Fanny, but she did not stand up and Alec thought that it was perhaps because her mother was dead, and that the noise in the organ was perhaps her mother's voice, it was so like her own; but Annie told him that the reason Cousin Fanny did not stand up at the hymns was her varicose veins, and that she was a perfect martyr to them. And Cousin Fanny told him that the noise in the organ was called the Vox Humana, which was a Latin name, because it sounded so like a very beautiful human voice.

One day Alec and the Watsons had to say a piece of poetry and it was about a dog called Gelert who saved a little boy's life, and his master killed him by mistake. And Alec said that the poetry was all wrong, because Gelert was still alive and slept on a sack in Cousin Fanny's kitchen. And the Watson's all laughed at him, because they knew the poetry must be true, since it was in a book. And after that there was a time when Alec was very ill, and the brass knob at the foot of his bed used to grin at him like a mischievous monkey, and queer people used to come into his room and chatter, and when the blue blind was down over the window he saw words printed on it in capital letters that he couldn't read, and faces looking at him through it, and he thought he was going for a walk with the Watsons, and they all vanished and an impewdent little man came out from behind a milestone and jumped over his head. And the impewdent little man followed Alec home and he *would* jump over his head, but Gelert came out of the kitchen and ate the impewdent little man up. And Alec felt quite well again, and looked round, and there was Cousin Annie sitting beside his bed. And he said to her: "There was such and impewdent little man, and he *would* jump over my head". And Cousin Annie went to the door and said something to somebody outside, and presently Cousin Fanny came in, and when she saw how well he was she cried, and knelt down beside him and said a little prayer, and then she went downstairs and sent a telegram to his father and mother in India, which Annie said was the first telegram that had gone out of that house for twenty years. And the wonderful thing was that Alec found that he had been ill for such a long time that the Queen's Birthday was over, and it was June, and he knew he was going to go on living forever. And Cousin Fanny told him that she and Annie had been in the room with him, turn about, the whole time he was ill.

After his illness Alec was not strong enough for lessons, and Cousin Fanny said he might play in any part of the house, except the bathroom because there was a hose-thing there that would squirt water in little tiny drops all over the room and into the passage, and she showed him many beautiful things. There was a picture of her father, his Uncle Archie, who had been a General in India, sitting on a horse with a native servant holding the bridle so that the horse shouldn't move until the picture was finished. And there was a little picture of a lady with her hair dressed very high on her head, who would have been Cousin Fanny's mother if she had only lived, but she had died out in India when she was still quite young and Uncle Archie had married Cousin Fanny's real mother after that. Cousin Fanny didn't seem very sad about Uncle Archie, but that was because he had died so long ago that even Annie didn't remember him, but the maid who was there then had told her that he used to use the most terrible language, because he had been so much in India and in the Mutiny. Annie had come to the house when Cousin Fanny was still a little girl with her mother, and then her mother was very sad all the year round because Uncle Archie was dead. And there was another picture, of Cousin Fanny's mother, but it was covered with a black curtain, because Cousin Fanny thought it was wrong to look at people's pictures when they were dead, only one day when Elizabeth was dusting the room she moved the curtain, and Alec saw the picture, and it was quite a young lady with a bare neck and bare arms and a flower in her hand. And the lady smiled at Alec, so she could not have been sad when the picture was painted. And there was a big fan on the wall like a peacock's tail; only it was hard like wood, and there were little mirrors at the ends of the feathers. And there was another picture of people dancing under a tree, which Cousin Fanny said was very precious, because her mother had bought it from a man who sold pictures. And there was an Indian cabinet full of things made of mother-of-pearl: a card-case and a needle-case and a thimble and a thing for winding silk, and a lot of other things (but Cousin Fanny couldn't remember what they were for) and counters that did for playing games. And the elephants with little castles on their backs, and the white bishops were like a lady Cousin Fanny knew, so that Alec wanted to laugh when the lady came to call, which she often did on Thursdays, and wanted to bring out one of the white bishops to show her how like her it was; and they all stood upon little carved stands except the red queen who had broken her stand, and had a lump of red sealing wax underneath her instead, which made her bob backwards and forwards when you put her on the board. And that always made Alec laugh too. But Cousin Fanny couldn't remember who had put the sealing-wax under the red queen. And the red king and a lot of the pawns were missing, so that when Alec played chess with Cousin Fanny they just used a common set of wooden chessmen. And in the corner of the room there was a big piano, and Alec used to lift the lid and play a few notes, and when he let the lid fall Cousin Fanny would look up from her chair and say: "Gently, dear!" And Alec thought of a great joke, and he used to lift the lid and play a note very loud and then pretend to let the lid fall, so that Cousin Fanny should look up and say: "Gently, dear!" when he had the lid in his hands all the time. But sometimes the lid did fall and hurt his finger, and then he would pretend nothing had happened, and go down to the kitchen and tell Annie, and she would go to a tin box on a shelf on the dresser which had a picture on it of kittens playing with cherries, and give him a handful of sultanas.

There was a garden behind the house, in which he was allowed to play on really fine days. It was not a very big garden, but some of the flowers were interesting, especially the Canterbury bells because they were like real bells, and the double daisies because they were like little red doormats, only round. And in the corner was a barrel for rainwater, and an old kennel in which Gelert used to sleep long ago, and Alec thought that had perhaps been when Cousin Fanny's mother was alive, because there wasn't room for Gelert in the house. But when he thought of Cousin Fanny's mother sleeping on an old sack on the kitchen floor, he laughed, it was so absurd; and Annie told him that Cousin Fanny's mother had died long before Gelert was a puppy even. The birds in the garden were

called starlings, and they used to eat the porridge Annie threw out
of the scullery window after everybody had had breakfast.

IV.

Alec had had two more birthdays at Cousin Fanny's when his mother
came home from India because she had not been at all well. She
was surprised to see what a big boy Alec had grown, and told
Cousin Fanny that she would never have known him. And Cousin
Fanny said: "Then I hope you'll let him stay with me". But presently
his mother told Alec that they were going away together, and a
lady was coming with them who, Annie told him, was called Madam-
as-well. Madam-as-well was very tall and came from Brussels, and
she did not speak very much except in French, so Alec would have
to learn French, to talk to her. He did not like Madam-as-well at
first, but Cousin Fanny said: "She's a Protestant, and that's always
something to be thankful for". So afterwards when Madam-as-well
was angry with him and boxed his ears, he remembered that she
was a Protestant, and was thankful, though he didn't know what a
Protestant was. Sometimes she was angry all day, except when they
were having their meals with Alec's mother, and she would tell
Alec that never in any of the families she had been with had she
ever seen such a little pig of a boy. But when she told him about
the families she had been with, he didn't think they could have been
very nice either, even a family called the Brombeers, who always
wore silk next to the skin. One day she gave him a little figure of
a boy, which she said was a copy of a very famous statue in Brussels,
but Alec's mother saw it and took it away; and she scolded Madam-
as-well, and Madam-as-well scolded Alec and sent him to bed
without the glass of milk and the biscuit he always had. And then
one night Alec's mother heard him crying when Madam-as-well
was downstairs having her supper, and came in and asked what was
the matter, and Alec only cried more and said: "I wish I had never

been born". And his mother whispered (but he could hear her): "This is the last straw", and sat down beside him and put her arms around him till he fell asleep. And when he woke up in the morning Madam-as-well had gone away, and very soon he had forgotten all about her.

V.

Before Alec's mother went back to India she took him to a real school where he was to be a boarder, and only go to Cousin Fanny's for the holidays. And when he went back the house seemed much smaller, though the things in it were nice still, but only because they were things he remembered long ago. And Cousin Fanny was quite stupid at times, because she could not understand what he was talking about. On the first day of the holidays she asked: "Are there any boys at school younger than you, Alec?" and he thought for a minute and said: "Do you mean boarders?" but then she was quite puzzled and didn't seem to know whether she meant boarders or the whole school, because of course some of the day-boys were heaps younger than Alec. So he changed the subject and talked to her about football, but she did not seem to be able to understand about that either. And at last she asked him: "Have you said how d'ye do to Annie yet?" He had, at the front door, but he went downstairs to get away from Cousin Fanny, and Annie gave him a great welcome, pretending she had to stand on tiptoe to see his face, he was such a great big boy; and Alec was pleased, because he was still a very little boy at school. And Annie showed him a cake she had been baking as a surprise for him and Cousin Fanny at teas, but now it would only be a surprise for Cousin Fanny; and she gave him a shilling that she had in a funny little purse that she said was made of mole-skin. Alec would rather have had the purse, because he could have swopped it, when he went back to school, for things that were worth more than a shilling, but he didn't say so, of course, to Annie. And Gelert was pleased to see him too, but he only thumped his tail on the floor, because he was such an old dog now that he didn't get up when people came in. And Alec was rather glad, because he had never liked the smell of Gelert's breath when he came to the table and leaned his chin on it, though Cousin Fanny said Gelert was a great comfort to her. Next time Alec came home there was no Gelert and Annie told him that Gelert had had to be put away, and that he musn't speak about it to Cousin Fanny. But in the holidays after that Cousin Fanny had a little white dog that she had bought from a man in the street; and she seemed quite happy again, and the new dog barked all day long, which Gelert had never done.

Alec was able to teach Cousin Fanny a great many things that he had learned at school, and things the other boys had told him, but she did not seem very quick at learning, and he preferred to tell things to Annie, because she always knew somebody to whom exactly the same things had happened when she was a girl, and it was wonderful how small the world was. Although she was a great deal busier than Cousin Fanny, she always had time to listen to him, and very often she gave him a shilling as well. But once he was quite waxy with her. He had been reading The Three Musketeers at school, and had read part of Twenty Years After in the holidays; and they were both jolly good, he thought. One evening, when Cousin Fanny had gone out to a meeting, he went into the dining-room and found his old Mademoiselle sitting there and Annie giving her a cup of tea. It seemed that Mademoiselle had been before this to see Cousin Fanny, and had told her how poor and deserving she was, and Cousin Fanny had been helping her. Alec did not remember her face, but she said at once that she would have known him anywhere and that he was the cleverest boy in the world. So he thought he would be polite, and said to her: "Est-ce que vous connaissez les livres de Monsieur Alexandre Dumas, Mademoiselle?" But she looked quite shocked and said: "But they are novels, they are not books for little boys". And Annie seemed puzzled, so

Mademoiselle explained to her about the books, and she shook her head and said she had heard of them. And Alec knew perfectly well she hadn't, and thought they were a pair of stupid women, and left the room.

VI.

Soon after his tenth birthday Alec heard that his mother was coming to live with Cousin Fanny, because the War had broken out in South Africa, and his father had to go to it, to fight with the other Battalion of the Regiment, which had come home when his Battalion went out to India. Alec was very proud of his father, and wore a button on the lapels of his coat with General Buller's head on it, except on Sundays; and soon he knew the names of all the places in South Africa where the War was being fought. But when he got back to Cousin Fanny's at Christmas he found his mother quite anxious, and every time the doorbell rang she started, and if it was a telegraph boy she hurried out of the room. Cousin Fanny was very sad about the War, which she thought was wicked, only she did not like to say so before Alec's mother; but when she and Alec were alone she shook her head and said in a very quiet voice that war was a great wrong, and Alec argued with her and said: "But not this War, Cousin Fanny!" But she still thought that all wars were wrong, and so Alec said: "What about the Mutiny?" because Uncle Archie had been a General in that. And she said: "The Mutiny was different, dear", though Alec didn't see why. But Annie liked the War, and had shaken her fist through the railings at a man who lived near and was suspected of being a pro-Boer. And in the winter after that, when the Queen died, she took the tea out of the tin that had the Queen's picture on it, and kept it afterwards in another tin with a picture of General Baden-Powell. And the tin with the Queen on it was put in the middle of the mantelpiece, next to a china dog which Alec had given Annie once when he was a little boy, to pretend it was her birthday. It seemed dreadful to Alec that the Queen should be dead, and he could never get used to hearing people singing: "God save the King", though of course there had been Kings in England before the Queen. But when the new stamps came out with the King's head on them he saved up enough pocket money to buy a whole set of them unused, except the higher values, which weren't stamps at all, really. Then his father came back from South Africa, and the Colonel had got a C.M.G and the Adjutant had got the D.S.O., and he had only got a brevet, which even Cousin Fanny said was a shame, though she didn't know what a brevet was and couldn't understand when Alec explained to her; but his father said it had been like that all round. And he took a house near the barracks where the Regiment had gone, at Aldershot, and Alec used to go there for his holidays, and some of the subalterns taught him to ride; so that it was a long time before he saw Annie or Cousin Fanny again.

VII.

Something that was said about Cousin Fanny finding things difficult now made Alec discover that she had been getting money from his pater all the time that he had been with her, which made him furious. Of course it had been jolly decent of Cousin Fanny to have him, though it had been rather slow having to spend one's hols in a poky little house with two old women and a mongrel dog, but that made it all the more beastly that Cousin Fanny should have needed to be paid to take him. He had always supposed she was fond of him, and he remembered how she used sometimes to take him on her knee when he was quite a kid, and ask him: "Whom do you love best, Alec?" and he had to say: "God;" and when she asked: "And next best?" he said: "Father and Mother in India," and when she said again: "And *next* best?" then he used to wait a little, to make her anxious, and hide his face on her arm, and say in a loud voice: "Cousin Fanny!" and then she was pleased. And all the time she had been taking money for him like a woman in a shop. He didn't know whether he hated her more for taking the money or his pater for offering it. Then he discovered that his pater had not very much money, and that when everything had been paid for there was very little left over; and he made up his mind when he grew up to be careful about money, and not to spend very much on things, as it was often difficult to get more.

VIII.

After his governor had left the Service, he and Alec's mother went abroad one Easter because of his sciatica, which was troubling him, and Alec said he didn't mind spending the holidays with Cousin Fanny. He rather liked the house this time, it was so full of things that reminded him of himself, and Cousin Fanny seemed younger than he remembered her, though Annie had shrivelled up like a little withered potato, and the white dog was very fat and always choking on the carpet, until he had to let it out. He and Cousin Fanny had dinner every evening with a woman called Miss Padge, who had come to live there as a paying guest, and Alec put on his black suit and pumps and a stick-up collar and a black bow tie, and Cousin Fanny had ordered in a lot of lemonade in blue syphons as a treat for him, and was quite shocked when he told her that they got beer at school. But Miss Padge only said, in a knowing voice: "Boys will be boys, Miss Fanny," which was the sort of thing she was always saying. Alec didn't like Miss Padge because she always flattered Cousin Fanny and, called her, "Miss Fanny", like a servant; but when Miss Padge went out to a lecture in the evening, which she often did to improve her mind, he and Cousin Fanny were quite happy together by themselves, and he used to play the piano to her, and she unlocked a rosewood cabinet and brought out a whole pile of songs that she used to sing long ago, and they sang them

together. Cousin Fanny sang: *We met, 'twas in a crowd*, but it always
made her very sad, because she had known someone like that when
she was a girl, whom her mother hadn't cared about. Alec sang *Ich
grolle nicht*, and several more of Schumann's songs, which a friend
of his sang at school, and he tried to sing *Erlkönig*, but the accom-
paniment was too difficult for them; besides, he didn't really under-
stand German, only what Cousin Fanny told him. And he read her
a lot of the poetry he had discovered in the library at school, and
she liked most of it very much, and he thought she had a great
deal more sense than most of the masters, who read nothing but
Wisden's Almanac, and thought poetry effeminate. She told him
that she had once nearly met Browning, at a friend's house, and
that he had been the last of the great poets, but Alec said, what
about Swinburne, who was still alive. Cousin Fanny had never heard
of Swinburne, and didn't seem to see the beauty of the poems Alec
could remember off-hand. But one day, when she was resting
because of the east winds (only Alec thought she said "These twins"
at first, and wondered who on earth the twins could be), he read
her *The Triumph of Time*, which he had copied out into a big note-
book with *Dolores* and *Sister Helen* and some poems from *The Defence
of Guenevere*; and she had to admit that *The Triumph of Time* was
very wonderful. And he thought of reading her *Dolores*, but he was
afraid it might shock her, so he read her William Morris's *Golden
Wings* instead, but she didn't care much for that. The only thing
was, Miss Padge always coming in and interrupting them, and one
morning at breakfast Miss Padge said: "I heard you from my room
yesterday, Miss Fanny; you were playing *so* beautifully!" when it
had been Alec who was playing, and he played simply rottenly, he
knew, because there was a chap at school who really could play;
and he thought Miss Padge was an old fool. He couldn't imagine
why Cousin Fanny kept her in the house, until she told him that
Miss Padge was very poor and couldn't afford to live anywhere else
like a lady. But he said that Miss Padge wasn't a lady, at which
Cousin Fanny sighed and said that we should never judge others,

and that Miss Padge had been a very earnest worker until her health gave way. Alec supposed that Cousin Fanny herself was probably too poor to be able to live like a lady without what she got from Miss Padge, and he felt very sorry for her and hoped that his governor was making it really worth her while to have him for these holidays.

One morning at breakfast Miss Padge asked whether Alec had been out to wash his face in the dew, and he couldn't think what she meant until she reminded him that it was the first of May; and he thought that May had something special to do with Cousin Fanny, but he couldn't remember what it was, and she didn't seem to remember either. But that afternoon in the drawing-room the sunlight fell on the picture of the girl in a ball-dress with a flower in her hand, and he remembered that this was the picture of Cousin Fanny's mother, which had always been covered with a black curtain because Cousin Fanny's mother was dead. And then he remembered that May was the month in which Cousin Fanny's mother had died, and that Cousin Fanny used always to be very sad then. And Miss Padge came in and began trying to tell him about the choirboys at Oxford on May morning, which made him furious because he had a friend who had gone up to Magdalen that year, and anyhow she had no business to talk about Oxford as if she'd invented it. A day or two later he went back to school, and Cousin Fanny gave him a pound, which he didn't quite like to take if she was so poor, except that he needed it, really, more than she did, and Miss Padge gave him a sacred picture framed in fir-cones, which she said she had got once in Bavaria. He went into the kitchen on his way to the cab, and Annie gave him a huge cake which she had baked for him, and told him he could eat grass off the top of her head now. This made him laugh, because she was almost bald. But he said it was jolly decent of her to have made him the cake.

IX.

He hadn't been near the place for years when he found himself posted
to a Service Battalion of his father's old Regiment, which was in
camp a few miles from where Cousin Fanny lived. He was there for
a couple of months, and twice a week he went over and had a hot
bath, and stayed to dinner with Cousin Fanny. The bath-room was
fearfully old-fashioned, with a brass thing on a tube, like a garden
hose, to spray yourself with, but most of the holes were stopped up,
and when you turned on the cold tap a trickle of hot water came
out of it. Still, it was better than having a bath outside his tent, in
the rain. His cousin had grown very small, and so wrinkled that when
she smiled her face was almost wicked, and he supposed that she
must be at least seventy. The first day he went over, she asked him:
"Have you been in to see Annie; your 'Cousin Annie', as you used
to call her?" He had forgotten all about Annie, but he ran down at
once to the kitchen and burst in; and Annie didn't know him at first,
and walked round him like a dog, to see who it was. Then she said:
"Well, you're a gentleman now!" and they both laughed, and he put
his stick and gloves on the table and lifted her onto it and told her
she could eat the grass off the top of his head. And she showed him
all the tin boxes with tea and rice and things in them, and a little
china dog she said that he had given her that stood beside a tin box
with a hideous picture of Queen Victoria at the time of the first
Jubilee. Alec wondered how old Annie was, remembering that she
had come to the house when Cousin Fanny was a child. Then he
went up to the drawing-room again and had tea with Cousin Fanny,
who asked if he thought the war was really a just war, because she
hated all wars, buts he hoped this one might be just. So he told her
all the things he had heard about the war, and they both became
very serious. And before he went back to camp she gave him a crucifix
which she had been asked to buy by an indignant gentlewoman, who
was Irish; and said that she didn't like to wear it herself, but perhaps
he would carry it in his pocket.

Before he went out to France he came over for a day, and said good-bye to them, and kissed them both, and promised to write. And Annie called out after him as he was going down the path to the gate: "I wouldn't go and fight for those Servians, Mr Alec. That's the second couple they've murdered." Which was her way of looking at it. And Cousin Fanny said that they would pray for him every day the war lasted, at Prayers, as well as in their own prayers. This made him feel very solemn, so she asked him timidly whether he still remembered the German songs they used to sing together; and they went to the rosewood cabinet and got out the volume of Schumann, and Alec sang *Ich grolle nicht* and *Erlkönig* and several others, and she sang *Du bist wie eine Blume* in a very quavery voice; and they tried to sing *Die Grenadier*, but he had to stop.

X.

One evening Alec's company came out of the trenches into billets in a half-ruined village which was already full of refugees from the other side of the line. In a room in which he and his subalterns had their dinner an old woman was sitting by the stove, turning over a rosary in her hands while tears rolled down her cheeks; and every now and then she sighed. She took no notice of the officers and Alec wondered why she stayed in the room, as they were making rather a noise, until he realised that there was no other room in the world where she could go. When one of them mentioned the name of the village through which their last trenches had run, she looked up with a start, and when Alec spoke to her told him that that was her village, and asked him if he had seen her house, which she tried to describe. There were no houses left within miles of the place, but he told her as gently as he could what a pretty village it was, and assured her that she would soon be safe at home again. While he was talking to her his company runner came in from Battalion headquarters with the Orders. The runner was a little old man, over fifty, who had been a poacher all his life, and could find his way to places he had never heard of before on the darkest nights and under heavy fire. He had always reminded Alec of somebody, and to-night as he looked at him he saw that the runner, who was warming his hands over the stove, was just like his cousin's old cook, Annie, and the old woman in the chair with her look of hopeless sadness, was like his Cousin Fanny herself. And he remembered that they were both praying for him, and made up his mind to write to them both that evening, and was looking in his haversack for paper and envelopes when another messenger came from headquarters inviting him to play poker with the C.O., Quartermaster and Chaplain. And next morning the Battalion marched back into a training area to prepare for the Spring offensive, in which half the officers and more than a third of the men were killed or wounded. Which kept one busy.

XI.

While he was at the base Alec had a long letter from his cousin, which made him cry because his arm hurt like the devil, and he remembered he had promised to write to her two years before. A V.A.D came past and stopped to tidy his bed (which hurt him even more), and pretended not to see that he was crying, but smiled at him because she supposed that he was in love and had just got a letter from his girl. Cousin Fanny had moved into a smaller house, and Annie had left, because the stairs were a difficulty, and had gone to live by herself in a town about ten miles away. She gave him Annie's address, and hoped that when he was in England, and able to get about, he would go and see her. He thought a great deal about Annie, and wondered how on earth she was managing to live. Cousin Fanny, he remembered, had never had a cheque-book in her life; or a latchkey, for that matter. When she wanted to take money out she used to write to New Square – which meant the office of her mother's solicitors – and about three days later a five pound note would arrive in a registered envelope. This she gave to Annie for the housekeeping, and Annie gave back whatever Cousin Fanny might want to spend on herself. Alec thought that he had heard that she paid Annie twenty pounds a year, and he supposed that Annie must have saved something out of that, though he could not imagine how. He made up his mind to send her a handsome present when his wound gratuity came. But by that time he was in London, and able to go out of hospital; and he found his expenses were very heavy, and whenever he thought, at night, as he lay awake, of sending something to Annie he always seemed to get a letter next morning reminding him that his account was overdrawn.

XII.

Some time after the war, Alec, who had been staying with friends in the country, received orders to appear before a Medical Board in the town in which Annie had gone to live. To be in time for the Board he had to arrive there overnight, and put up at a hotel. He had Annie's address still in his pocket-book and next morning, after the Board had examined him, he went to find her. The house was a tenement in a very poor quarter, and after he was inside it occurred to him that he had never known Annie's other name. As he was standing in the passage and had almost decided to go back to his hotel, a woman came downstairs who looked at him curiously and said: "You'll be Master Alec; have you come to see Annie?" This was distinctly odd; but the woman led him up to the top floor of the house and opened a door, and then stood in the doorway with her apron pressed to her face. Alec went into the room, which was very small, and frousty with the smell of extreme poverty. The ceiling sloped upwards from the opposite wall, with a cracked skylight facing him, under which a saucer had ben placed on the floor to catch the rain. The only chair stood by the fireplace, the grate in which had been closed up with bricks so as to leave only an inch or two for fuel. A few clothes hung on nails. A cup and saucer, two plates, a knife, a fork and a big and a little spoon were arranged on a dresser in one corner. In the other corner was an iron bed, which seemed to Alec familiar somehow, and the woman went across to it and pulled down the blanket that was spread over the pillow. Then he saw Annie's face. She had died the evening before, while he was sitting at dinner in his tedious hotel, wondering what on earth he could do until bedtime. "She was always talking about Master Alec," the woman explained, and showed him a photograph tacked to the wall over the bed, of himself as a subaltern, which he had given to Cousin Fanny before he went to France. He looked round the room again, and saw on top of the dresser a little china dog which he remembered Annie's telling him he had given her once, years before, for her birthday or something, and a tin biscuit-box with a coloured picture of the old Queen on it, which (he remembered quite well) had been emptied of tea and put on the kitchen mantelpiece after the Queen's death. The woman who had brought him upstairs made some excuse and left the room; and Alec stood for a long time gazing at Annie's quiet face.

He had stood in this way by many of his most intimate friends in the last five years, had lain awake in hospital wards where someone or other died every night, had helped to bury brother officers and men of his own company, when the ground was frozen too hard for a pick to break it; but Annie dead; Annie to whim he had scarcely given a thought in all that time, was different. He knelt by the bed, sobbing, felt for her hard little hand and kissed it again and again, then rose and stooped over her face and kissed her shining forehead, smiling through his tears as he remembered her little joke about his eating grass off the top of her head. Her face had that slightly shocked expression that she used to put on when she saw him come running into the kitchen with his fingers crushed in the lid of his cousin's piano. He tiptoed across the room, took up the little china dog, and slipped it into his pocket. As he did so he wondered whether anyone else in all her eighty years had ever given Annie a present. This at least was to his credit. But on the other side, all the laborious, loving, ungrudging service of all those years, poured out for himself and other people without any question of their response to her. Miss – what was the woman's name? – Pudge, for instance; what had Miss Pudge – or Padge, was it? That sounded more likely – been to Annie but another mouth to be fed. Every single day since her childhood Annie had had to prepare all her own meals, and, until extreme old age, other people's as well. He thought of all the service that had been rendered him every day of his life, at school and in the army, and how easily he had taken it. What had he ever given Annie? Kisses, when he was little; and a china dog – and she had spent every moment when she was not in her kitchen by his bedside when he was ill. Why this was the bed he had been ill in. He could see its battered brass knob now grinning at him like a – what animal was it – a monkey? She had given him shillings, too, in his school holidays. How many times a year had he so much as thought of her since he had grown up? Had Cousin Fanny thought of her, in these last years, either? But then, what had he ever done for Cousin Fanny? At least he could break the news of Annie's death to her now. He left the house, telling the woman (whom he met again on the stairs) that he would return later and make all the arrangements for the funeral, and, after telegraphing to postpone his arrival at the house at which he was staying, hired a motor-car and drove to his cousin's new address. He found her sitting up in bed, wearing a pink flannel dressing-jacket which seemed to revive in him a memory so remote that he could make nothing of it. She was pleased to see him, but puzzled at first to know why he had so suddenly come. And he could not speak; until at last: "Cousin Annie's dead!" he cried out to her.

"Cousin Annie, dear?"

"Annie, your old cook."

"Oh!" His cousin seemed quite unmoved. Then, with a little twist of her mouth, she piped: "Well, we must all die some time, I suppose."

Alec had never imagined her to be utterly heartless. It was only after a minute of strained silence, when he saw the girlish face of her mother smiling down at her from the picture opposite the foot of her bed, that he realised that she, too, might be longing to be set free from the burden of life.

Published by T.S Eliot in the New Criterion
April and July 1926

THE VICTORIANS

I.

It was impossible for Lady Soulis, looking out that evening from the tower window, to see more than half a mile of the unfenced hill-road, illumined here and there obscurely by pools of rain-water; and, against the perceptible whiteness, a few sheep blotted. Now and again, in the valley, a lighted train passed through or lingered in Coldwaterford Station, audible rather than visible in the gathering mist. It had rained all day, as the way is there in Spring, and darkened early, and the river valley with the English hills beyond, was shut out of sight.

Those English hills, from which alarms traditionally sounded, had no longer – she thought with a miserable contentment, – any power to harm her. In the four centuries since they had sent forth a panoply to Scotland's ruin on Flodden Field, their malignant force had diminished; in the last four years, sending into her solitude the news that, one by one, her three sons' lives were taken, they had dealt their last blow. And yet seeing in the boys not men so much as her men, the heirs-male of her body, she felt uneasily that the vengeance was, perhaps, a just one: the punishment, delayed but certain, of her early sin. From this meditation she was recalled by the servants' entering; the candles and books were arranged, and, turning to her place at the table, she led her household in thanksgiving and prayer. Ending the appointed Portion of Scripture, she waited while all knelt around her, and then, in her clear tones of leadership, gave thanks for benefits received during the day, and prayed for members and friends of the household, absent now and perilously engaged in their country's service.

Some of the maids betrayed an easily stirred emotion, but the old lady's voice never faltered, and, committing her family to the

Peace of God, she rose to dismiss them for the night. Then, taking up her candle, she made her customary round of the bedrooms where her sons would never lie again: a duty solemnly performed, lest by inattention or neglect any insult should be offered to their memory. Alone she visited those rooms, which, while life remained in her, no stranger should ever enter. After her death, when the Canadian cousin came to inherit Hermitage, let him do what he might. She, until at the limit of her power she joined them, would be faithful.

To-night, as she went round, the impression was strengthened that recently in the rooms little adjustments had been made by hands other than her own. A loose sash in Hugo's window had rattled which, to-night examining it, she found carefully wedged; and in Kenneth's room there was a rearrangement of his boots, surely in the order in which he had liked them.

Her solemn duty performed, she returned to the tower room; and was surprised to find Bedlow, her butler, still standing by the door which gave upon the servants' quarters. He had come to her from an English family some months earlier, a few days before the news of Kenneth's death in France. He had been kind to her then, she remembered, as kind as any stranger could have been in her unapproachable sorrow. Since then, living people had meant daily less to her, and although she saw him daily she could scarcely have described his face. Now, as she stood awaiting an explanation of his presence she was puzzled by something suggestive in his appearance. Facing him on the other wall was her father's portrait, of which he seemed to have copied instinctively the pose, the stern expression of face and clenching hands, the repressed but dominant air of virtue. And in his eyes there was some even more intimate memory.

While she felt that an explanation was due from him, curiosity impelled her to speak the first, and "Did you ever see any of 'my sons?" her tongue uttered drily.

"Yes, my lady."

"Which one?" – after a pause in which several questions might come up for answer, she went on.

"All, my lady."

This made her pause, for her sons, differing in their ages and in their inclinations, had never kept much together: she looked at him fixedly, weighing his answer. His voice, steeped and stiffened as it was in respectful formality, recalling suddenly the severity of her father's, it was almost timidly that she again addressed him: "And how came that about?"

"By chance, merely, my lady: it happens that I have been in service, one time and another, in houses where the each of the gentlemen visited. It is nearly thirty years since I first saw the Master of Soulis, when I was second footman to Sir Diggory Rolleway at Hampton Dumpton. Your ladyship may remember the family." – her head moved slightly – "He came down there every year for the partridges, and I can well remember looking after him. Your ladyship's photograph was always on his dressing-table."

"Indeed!" Surprise forced the ejaculation from her. The Master, heir to her peerage, had long been the most distant of her sons, had contributed the least share of the very little affection she knew herself to have won from them. He had lived chiefly in London, employed in the service of some arid political theory whose application to unknown social conditions had never interested her. He had come home, when war began, to recruit a company of Infantry from their own border country, and had been leading that company on to the bloody battlefield of Loos. Hugo, his next brother, had died some month before the war from an accident, while hunting in Leicestershire. Kenneth, by many years the youngest and therefore, perhaps, the dearest, though the most wayward also and least home-loving of the three, had grown up from Winchester and had served for a few years in the Rifles when war began. After that, only in one spell of leave had he found time to visit Hermitage, before he came there forever as the latest memory of an extinguished line. He was the handsomest of her boys, and not yet twenty-seven, commanding his Battalion, and generally admired and trusted when, not even in any historic encounter, he had been killed by a casual shell 'about two hundred yards,' they had told her, 'from the cross-roads'. These memories were confused in her mind as she went on to ask "And the others?"

"I was temporary butler, my lady, to Mr Mompesson, when Hugo came down there—"

"The last time?"

"Yes, my lady. I attended the funeral. He was speaking of your ladyship when they carried him into the house."

"And Mr Kenneth?"

"Ah, I knew him very well:" was it some imperfection in her own sight that made the butler's eyes seem to swim in tears? – "Many and many a time he came to stay in the country, where I was, – and in London to: I was able to do him a service once; I think your ladyship would find that he remembered me."

"He did not mention it," she said coldly. How little he had mentioned. Her isolation in the presence of a man who had known all three of her sons, whom they – if one could be said to 'know' a friend's butler, – had known in turn, was overpowering. Hardly able to breathe she sat down, her hands folded on the table. Bedlow too had his memories. The danger into which young Kenneth had let himself be drawn, the adroitness and patience with which Bedlow had saved him from an imminent social ruin, and the boy's quick and lasting gratitude were not things he could even hint to his mistress; but, as he stood pondering them, his professional stiffness melted, he rose up naturally, freely before her, and his likeness to her father surged again into her numb consciousness.

"And then you came to me," she began kindly, "but I think you are not a Scotsman."

He faced her with "I understand that my mother was from this country."

"Indeed. But you were not born here?"

So she must have it. "I was born near London, my lady, in the village of Hardenchurch."

She dwelt on it for a moment; then, in a lighter tone, went on: "And why did you come to me?"

"Mr Kenneth had spoken to me very seriously about you, my lady. He thought that your ladyship was lonely down here, and when I read that your ladyship required a butler, I asked my mistress to recommend me."

Another question burned on her tongue, but she avoided its direct opening with "You are past military age, I think."

Again she must have it. "I was born in February, 1870, my lady."

"At Hardenchurch, you said."

"At Silver Cottage, Hardenchurch."

"Ah!" the involuntary sound escaped her, "Your parents lived there?"

"I never knew my parents. I was brought up in Hardenchurch by a Mrs Peach, who had money sent her for my maintenance. But I went into service as a boy."

"Is this Mrs Peach alive?"

"She has been dead for some years, my lady. She seemed in great distress before she died, and said she must tell me—"

"And did she tell you?"

"Yes, my lady."

"About your parents?"

"Yes."

"Then you know—" the prudence of a lifetime melted like wax on the flame of her excitement.

"I know."

"That I am your—"

"Mother!" The unaccustomed word rang out and shattered the brooding silence of the tower room. Lady Soulis rose and turned aside. The face of her father's portrait seemed to frown upon her in the uncertain light of her candle. Holding it steadily, she passed to the door, which Bedlow held open for her. From the passage without her voice came to him in the darkness.

"Good-night."

"Good-night, my lady."

II.

For a week their intercourse was purely formal. Each, when they met, maintained a reserve whose measure was set by the determination not to fall in any way short of the reserve practiced by the other. But one evening, as she paid her visit, a discreet sound in Kenneth's room proved to come from a kneeling figure, carefully dusting the long line of boots that spread out underneath one wall. Bedlow rose as she entered.

"Tell me," she began calmly, as though she had expected this meeting, "When did you see Kenneth?"

"When he was last on leave," the answer came quietly, as from an equal. "he came down to us, and he talked a great deal to me."

"Of what?"

"Of himself, and what he would do when the war ended. He felt he ought to leave the service and live here: there was a lot he could do here, he said."

She had not heard of this, and stiffened for a moment in her proper pride.

"I can do every thing here, as I did long before Kenneth was born."

"He only wanted to help you here, to carry out your orders. He had not done himself justice in the army."

"But he did brilliantly,"

"Yes." Bedlow was silent, remembering the painful confidences of a weak boy, who in the dark intervals between his moments of triumph was conscious of his weakness. "This was home, you see, and he had duties here, to you and to the place. I was to come with him." He added, after a pause.

"To come with him!" she had a moment of horror.

"As his own man. But your butler was old, he told me, and would take a pension when the war ended."

"Then he never knew?"

"Oh, my lady!" Bedlow was at once the butler, but a butler shocked into self-expression. "How could I have told him?"

"True. He would not have believed you."

"He would never have been asked to."

"You would have lived here and said nothing, ever, to me even?"

"No, no: you do not understand. I loved Kenneth."

"Loved him?"

"He was only a boy when he first came to us; – he was still a boy at the end, last year. But I told you I had done him a service. I would do the same for any one, and it was not a thing we ever spoke of afterwards; but it was not a thing we could ever forget, either, and he used to tell me all his troubles; – if you could see" he broke off "some of the letters he wrote me, from the war!"

She pondered it honestly for a minute, but could not understand, and so seized, rather, the urgent question of the moment. "And what are you going to do now?"

"Now?" he in turn questioned.

"You cannot stay on like this."

"I hoped I was giving satisfaction." – he smiled at the formula.

"Do you mean, you are willing to stay?"

"I am perfectly content, and if I have any duty, surely it is to remain with your ladyship now."

"I have lived alone for many years."

"And I hope to serve you for as many."

"No. I am an old woman now. I have no use for the years."

His hands silently deprecated her suggestion.

"You wish to remain as you are here?" she went on. "You would claim—"

"Nothing."

"When I am gone: my heir is, you know, a Canadian gentleman. He has not visited me yet, but—"

"I should be very happy to remain in his service, if it were his wish, and yours."

"No; it is unthinkable!" she said, firmly grasping at one the definite impossibility among the crowding disastrous possibilities of the situation. Her son might not continue her line but he should never do service to a stranger in her place.

"I am at your ladyship's disposal."

"Very well. I must think over what you have told me. I shall go to bed now. You will come to the justice room in the morning."

"After your ladyship's breakfast?"

"At nine o'clock"

"Very good, my lady."

"Good night, my lady."

"Good night," – she thought for a moment – "Walter." Her hand went out towards him,

"Good-night," he bowed stiffly until his lips touched it, "Mother."

III.

Neither baroness nor butler slept easily that night, distracted as each was by the complexities of their newly established relation. To her he was still primarily the butler, and Commonsense urged, 'Dismiss him'. Conscience hesitated, while Motherhood pleaded that, at least, he be allowed to remain in the house. 'How much does he know?' Commonsense questioned. Conscience blushed. 'Of course he will make a claim.' Commonsense continued. 'He is welcome,' sighed Motherhood. 'Think of the scandal' argued Commonsense. 'But I cannot dismiss him' answered Conscience. Commonsense reflected that if he were aggrieved by an unjust dismissal, he might provoke a worse scandal. And so Catherine Douglas, Baroness Soulis of Hermitage, had the last word. "We will speak quite frankly in the morning. Merciful Father, forgive me my trespasses, and shew me the right."

Bedlow's reflections were simplified by his knowing only a part of his own story. He had been already for some years a butler, highly respected in several families when he had learned his mother's name and rank. And by an unaccountable lapse of memory his Mrs Peach, who had confessed to him on her deathbed her long concealment of the story, had named his mother but not his father, and the omission weakened any claim he might have felt bound to put forward.

He had learned that by the Law of Scotland he could apply for a Declarator of Marriage between his parents, by which he would become automatically Master of Soulis. But, during Kenneth's lifetime, his keen affection for this strangely remote and yet more strangely intimate brother put out of consideration any claim which might infringe that brother's acknowledged rights; and, even now, he was loth to take any step that, by establishing his own legitimacy, would denounce his dead brothers as bastards. Mentally he was of the generation in whose service he had grown up, and shared to the full his mother's horror of scandal. Hermitage was a quiet house in a remote parish, but, even though he won house lands and title by litigation, he could never enjoy them. How could he keep servants who would have seen his face and his mother's, vilely portrayed in daily newspapers. He would claim nothing beyond his right to remain in his mother's house as her servant, at least while she lived. It was an old house, that had belonged for centuries to his ancestors; and he, who had never known so much as a mother until he came there, loved it already more than, he felt, had any of his brothers. It was proper for him to stay.

In the morning Bedlow found his mistress at her table in the justice room, from which she governed the secular affairs of her small estate. She rose as he entered, and came towards him with something in her hand.

"Good-morning," she greeted him nervously. "I wish you to take one of these." – and she held out an old and discoloured box of cigarettes. He drew back in surprise, for he had heard of this box from Kenneth, and could estimate the astonishing compliment that she had decided to pay him. Ten years earlier, the King of England, journeying northwards to figure briefly at Holyroodhouse as King of Scots, had arranged to take luncheon with one whom it was fitting that he so honour, and Lady Soulis had prepared her house for his reception. After the meal, she was warned, His Majesty would expect a cigarette, and, although it was her boast that no tobacco had ever yet been burned within the walls of Hermitage, she yielded to superior judgement, and instructed her lawyer in Edinburgh to procure a box of the best kind. The King came by road with his gentlemen, and courteously accepted the hospitality of her table. He welcomed her as a friend almost of his own generation, and recalled seeing her father in the early days of Balmoral. Watching his plate, she rose at length and unlocked a cupboard, from which she drew out the abhorrent box and laid it open before him. He took a cigarette, and, as he turned aside to light it, she quickly removed the box, and locked it again in the cupboard, where it had stayed until to-day. Kenneth had told the story as much from pride in his mother's firmness of principle as from amusement at the discomfiture of the King's fellow travellers, who had, also, expected cigarettes. And this was the amazing box, that had come forth as out of a sepulchre to do honour to him, to Bedlow the butler, the foundling. He collected himself, and looked up to see his mother still standing before him, the cigarettes in her hand. Very reverently he took the box from her and opened it.

'Will you please to sit down." She ordered, pointing to a chair opposite her own. He obeyed, and, by a happy intuition, held the cigarette in his hand, unlighted.

"I have thought a great deal," she began, "over what should be done; and I must first tell you that part of your story which you probably do not know. My mother died when I was born; and I was brought up in this house, an only child, by my father and his sister. She was a widow, whose only son had gone to live in Canada, and it is his grandson who must succeed me here. I was eighteen when your father first came over: from Northumberland." she looked out of the window, which the English hills still morosely darkened. "My father could not abide him, but I had seen very few young men, and I was ready to listen to him. At last, in May, when my father was gone to the General Assembly in Edinburgh, and my aunt was confined to her room, your father came to Hermitage and pressed me to become his wife. I consented, and went with him to Berwick, where we stayed. Next day we were to go by train to London; but my heart failed me and I returned here. We had very faithful servants then, and nothing was ever said of my absence. My father returned, but shortly after was seized with a fatal illness, and died before the New Year. And so I became my own mistress, and again your father came to me; and, this time, I accompanied him to England; for I knew then that you would very soon be born. But don't you see what a fatal scandal it would have made; I was in deep mourning, and could not be publicly married for a year. So your father found a quiet place for me at Hardenchurch; and there, when you were a fortnight old, I left you. I came home, and was married from this house a year later. Edward, my dear boy, came two years after you, and then Hugo, and Kenneth, my baby." In the emotion of her terrible confession she did not observe the equal emotion of her astonished son. In all his speculations on his paternity he had never reached the simple, obvious truth, that he was the child of his mother's husband. How preposterous – now that he regarded the virtuous old lady before him – was the base alternative. So there was no case for a Declarator of Marriage, no question of bastardising his brothers. He was legitimate, if not so from the hour of his birth, from the day of his parents' subsequent marriage. All his resolutions of the night-time faded in this searching new light.

"And so," he broke in boldly upon her confusion, "I am Master of Soulis."

"What do you mean?" she trembled.

"That your marriage made me legitimate – though you have all these years disowned me. Tell me, did you know – did you never care to hear that I was alive?"

"My dear," she dropped to a tone of apology strangely out of harmony with her rigorous nature, "I wanted to have you here, but after Edward was born your father persuaded me that it was impossible. The truth would have come out and I should never have been forgiven. We paid for your maintenance until you" – she hesitated at the mention of his servitude – "found employment; and after that he would never tell me what was become of you. I did not even know what surname they had given you, but you were christened Walter."

"Walter Douglas," he murmured, "Master of Soulis."

"No: not that."

"Yes; I claim that."

"But you cannot. Only think of the scandal. In my old age would you show me this injustice?"

"And I have suffered no injustice?"

She faltered. Then – "But you say you were happy."

"Happy enough as I was, when I did not know what else I might have been; but, after I knew, do you think I never felt the want of anything? I had grown up without father or mother, without a relative in the world, and, when I knew that your Kenneth, whom I cherished and protected with an elder brother's love, was indeed my brother, do you think I never minded that he must see me socially as a ventriloquist's dummy, an oddity of the servants' hall that it might amuse him to confide in. I wish now" he ended bitterly "that I had told him. He at least would have understood."

"Do not speak of such a thing. Why are you so changed since last night?"

"Last night" – he fell at once into the error, – "I did not know."

"Know what?"

He hesitated. "That my father was your husband."

She rose to her feet, her cold features coloured, and her eyes blazing with passion. "Oh, this is too much. After all these years you come back to insult me. So you conceived of me as a light woman, like one of those you have probably waited upon, in England. It is intolerable. You must leave me. I cannot possibly keep you here."

Bedlow controlled himself fiercely, and, almost speechless with pain, murmured, "Very good, my lady."

She left the room. After a moment he followed her, flinging first his cigarette into the empty fire-place.

IV.

For a month they went about their duties in silence, always contriving, without apparent avoidance of the other, not to be alone in each other's presence. In the world, of which they heard little, page after page of history was being filled. In France, the enemy had swept irresistibly forward, capturing men and guns, hills, rivers, towns, and, principally for Bedlow, the cross-roads where Kenneth's body lay. This news roused him from his dull melancholy to an active resentment of the evil forces that continuously beset him. In his hatred of the nation that had violated his brother's grave he merged a hatred more intense, because more concentrated, of the mother who had prevented him from playing his proper part in that brother's existence. She, meanwhile, seemed in that month to have lived through many barren years. Gradually, by successive delegations of her responsibility, she had withdrawn from the active life of the house, and stayed daily longer in her bedroom. There, coming apologetically before her one morning, he announced his intention of leaving her service with "a month's notice."

She gazed at him out of the dimness of her curtained bed, and answered with the calm question, "Why do you wish to leave me?"

"I intend to join the army, my lady."

"The army: but you are a man of eight and forty!"

"They have older men than me, now, in the army, my lady. Besides, when the young men are gone, older men must take their place."

"No, no; you cannot. I have formed other plans for you."

"You have, my lady?"

"I mean to acknowledge you now, here, as my heir."

He shrank from their old contention: "Would that be wise, my lady?"

"I have no time now to consider wisdom. I must set right this injustice while I still have the power. Give me that box." She pointed to a jewel-case covered in faded morocco, that stood on her dressing-table. He brought it to the smaller table by her bed, and watched her choose out the key. While she searched in the box, "I wrote yesterday," she added, "to Edinburgh. The lawyer will arrive shortly. You will see that he has his luncheon."

"Very good, my lady."

In the bottom of the box she had found a small sealed envelope, which she held out to him. "This is for you." she explained. "Keep it very carefully."

"I thank you, my lady."

When she had arranged and looked at the box, he restored it to her dressing-table; and then took his leave. He did not see her again.

V.

Mr Kirkpatrick Geddes, a Writer to His Majesty's Signet, walked up to Hermitage from the Coldwaterford Station, and was closeted for an hour with Lady Soulis. As he came out, Bedlow met him, and led him to the tower room, where a table was laid. Mr Geddes was not ashamed to be hungry after his journey, and fed heartily, half turning now and then as though to interrogate the butler who stood behind his chair. Looking up from a plate of bread and cheese, his eye met the painted gaze of the old Lord Soulis, and he smiled grimly. "Wonderful," He muttered, "how these old families replenish themselves."

"Most remarkable, sir." Bedlow assented.

The meal was interrupted by the housekeeper, who reported that her mistress had been found, unconscious in bed. Bedlow excused himself; he must send a groom for the doctor. Mr Geddes, after a polite expression of alarm took his seat again at the table, and cut himself another slice of cheese.

The doctor could pronounce only that life was extinct: the heart, long threatening, had at last failed. Had the dead lady been subjected to any recent strain or emotion? "Of course, the sad loss of her sons—" he murmured to Mr Geddes.

"The loss," the lawyer took it up. "I wonder."

The doctor signed a certificate and went out, leaving him alone. Presently he rang the bell.

"Allow me to congratulate your lordship!" he began.

"I do not understand you, sir." – the answer was solid.

"No! Well, the old lady confided everything to me this morning. It is fortunate for you that I arrived in time. Of course, I had a pretty shrewd suspicion of this before; my father told me the story as he knew it. Then we have a journal in the office of your father's, showing his itinerary to – to – Hardenchurch, do they call the place?"

Bedlow was silent.

"So that all we need to do now is to produce the certificate of birth: but what more evidence could a judge require than your portrait? D'you know, I thought at first, you were some imposter that had got a hold of her story, and come to trade on her conscience; but, man – my lord, I should say, the likeness: – oh, it's astounding."

"You rang, I think, sir," said Bedlow coldly.

"Don't you understand the situation? She told me you knew all about it. The poor lady we have just lost was your mother, and you are in consequence, let me see, the eighteenth Lord Soulis of Hermitage. An honoured race, let me tell you: – *atavis edite regibus.*"

As he met the butler's coldly respectful stare his confidence waned, to be revived by occasional glances at the portrait. "No doubt it is all very strange to you, I must be getting my train now, but you shall hear from me shortly." Bedlow followed him downstairs, and helped him into his coat. Then returning to the tower room he took the small envelope from his pocket, and broke its seal. Inside was a paper signed by his father and mother, and by two witnesses of their irregular marriage at Hermitage, in May 1869. Here was the easy proof which she had guarded all these years; of which she had never spoken, but which she had held so precious that only to his hands in the end would she confide it. He looked at it in silence for some minutes, then, laying it on the lawyer's empty plate, struck a match and watched the paper curl and shrivel and blacken, and whiten again and scatter in the little breeze that came from the hills.

VI.

It was a clear a beautiful day in late autumn. The war, which had called to Bedlow a few months earlier, was now ended, and the country was endeavouring to recover its strength and activity, and to welcome its defenders. Bedlow stood in the front door of Hermitage, watching the unfenced road from the village, on which a few sheep strayed. Presently a car appeared climbing the hill and drew up beside him, from which a young officer, in Canadian uniform, and a lady slightly older, of emphasised good looks, alighted. A new wedding-ring flashed on her well-groomed hand.

Bedlow received them with deference and ushered them into the house. In the justice room the young man paused, regarding the faded Douglas tartan with which its walls were lined.

"I reckon we must send an S.O.S to the decorators." He observed thoughtfully. "I can just about smell the flowers growing on my grave, in here."

"Really. I think it's all very picturesque and romantic," said the lady, as they climbed the tower stair; "and you say you're the eighteenth Lord!"

"It may be romantic, but it's not comfortable. However, we shan't be saying here that long, anyway. It's me for the gay metropolis."

The driver had given no hint that any luggage was to be removed from the car, and Bedlow gathered that the young couple were going on to make a tour of Scotland while the fine weather lasted. In twenty minutes they had seen all the house, and were once more in their car.

"Well, good-bye, Mr Mutt," said the officer; "and look after this old ruin until I may happen to require it. I should say you belonged to the house."

"Yes, my lord," answered Bedlow, "I belong to the house."

When the car had driven away, he stood there for a little, silent, smiling at something in his mind. Then he turned indoors.

CKSM 1919

Published in the London Mercury, August 1923

´ANT.´

It wasn't, I think, before his third or fourth appearance in the drawing room that Bracton was aware of her existence, so quiet a note, hardly the hum of a telegraph pole in her niece's gusty atmosphere, had she all the time been sounding. And seeking shelter one day from that boisterous weather in her corner while the crowded room shook with the discussion of some mixed hockey match of the last winter, he felt at the first sight of so old and faint a type that there would be no more than her name to be got, for him, out of their acquaintance or into hers than the reciprocal knowledge of his. She was, of course, the old, the original Miss Dentwood, aunt of the hilarious James and Bessie, and degraded, in the course of years into 'Miss Anna' by her niece's gradual mastery of the household. She had, he supposed, in some unimaginable childhood of the latter lady, been of domestic value there, ordered meals, invited guests, seen to things generally in the kitchen and laundry, arranged perhaps even the garden that still made Manticross the pleasantest among several agreeable baiting-places for a young man condemned to grow older in the professional life of Burbridge. If indeed the baiting-places weren't rather just in their professional life, in those office-hours which assumed quite an air of inertia between the pastimes, hockey or lawn tennis while the light lasted, bridge and pyramids when it failed, in all which one had to live strenuously up to the high standards of fun and nosiness set by Bessie Dentwood and her sister-amazons.

Horsley Bracton's connection, too recent still to be yet intense, had been formed that year on his arrival at the old headquarters there of Ducket's Banking Company, which his uncle had now absorbed into his larger London interests. With all the "Proprietor's of Ducket's" Bracton must soon or late become acquainted, but into the Dentwood household he had been precipitated by the commending letters, to both parties, of a Mrs Grogan, their married

Maggie and the wife of his old housemaster at school. This lady's affairs, her look of health and wellbeing, and her skill in catering for two score of hungry schoolboys, seemed at first the sole topic Miss Anna and he could reasonably have in common; and these once exhausted, the old lady persevered a silence which left him free until the tea should come to regard her with the curiosity her remoteness from the hearty scene inspired. She sat always, it seemed, in this dim corner, overarched by the two shelves of her small library; between the faded green of her silk costume and the faded blue of the wall-paper, the whiteness of her face and hands arrested the eye as might a group of chalk pits in the neighbouring downs. It was impossible, so beached were these members, to guess when – hard, indeed, to believe that at any time they had been animated by some flow, however restricted, of that vitality her niece and nephew had so richly inherited. Nothing, it struck him, would ever discolour those glowing cheeks or stiffen the athletic figures: but their current of life must have slipped quite past the aunt in whose pale eyes their regarded activities seemed to awaken no memories. With those eyes, whose pigment was exactly matched in the lavender ribbon of her old lace cap, she was almost constantly engaged, in the old phrase, in minding her book. The dozen or so of three-volumed novels he could make out on the shelves above them had each in its appointed season in her lectionary, which was relived and brightened by the monthly arrival between her hands of the *Regent Magazine*. "This is," she had indeed piped to him on their introduction, "a most interesting number of the *Regent*. I hope that you see it regularly." Fearing a loan, which she did not, however, press further, he gave an ambiguous answer. "We are here," she went on, "as you must have noticed, quite out of the way of things. But I gather more than you would think from these pages." At a loss here, for the *Regent*, in truth, he had always suspected, brought up as he had been by a careful widowed mother, of a certain flashiness, Horsley had turned sharply to the subject of her other niece, the kind old Miss Grogan of his schooldays.

One got with so little effort into Burbridge society that he hardly felt himself, in that quiet corner, to be still out of it nor to be any more drawn into it when, tea arriving, Miss Bessie Dentwood strode up to him. Loud, confiding, friendly she rang out in the old lady's ear her welcoming peal of "Don't, my dear man, let 'Ant'" – James and Bessie both shortened the diphthong – "in any way bother you. She had her tea quietly here, and we don't disturb ourselves. But I want you particularly to meet Ella Sawbridge. She and James are, of course, going to win our mixed doubles next month." Drawn or not, he was in the thick of things henceforward, and talked or listened to Miss Sawbridge an enormous girl in pink muslin, until he was decently able to take his leave of the party. In this act he seemed to surprise the others by crossing the room again to shake Miss Anna's hand. That was a ceremony he gathered about which, few people now, in Burbridge, bothered. She had always, they were dimly aware, been at Manticross, and would certainly be in her place still at their next call there, her retirement perhaps outraged by a too near approach of their harmless hilarities. She must indeed, – he approved the popular sentiment – tremble a little when the talk ran high in those endless channels of athletic history. Those thin temples must ache sometimes at a noisy bridge party, and no one, he guessed, would be noisier at Bridge than James Dentwood, though Bessie might be found more shrill. Yet – and though the weakest go to the wall – the high standard of Burbridge society must be maintained. Wasn't it kinder, then, to ignore, by withholding the frightening fingers of youth and strength, that quiet personality who had, so far as was known, no such social achievements of her own even to look back upon?

II.

It was, perhaps, with a paradoxical sense of fitness in conformity with his youth that he chose, for his next call at Manticross, the afternoon of Sir Humphrey Rolleway's garden party at Hampton Dumpton, to which he had by some easily pardonable error been left uninvited. James, in his unathletic hours Sir Humphrey's solicitor, was with Bessie so obviously at the moment breaking one record or another upon the baronet's lawns that Horsley confidently asked, and was admitted, to see Miss Anna. In her usual corner of the drawing room less prepared than usual to receive the searching social glare, she was as he entered the one remembered, recognisable object. He reached her, he vaguely knew, through a wilderness where kittens, "done in oils" upon a dozen cushions, and patterns of cornflowers or honesty branded by some hot implement upon as many tripod little stools, stood up to delay his passage; but these things had, in Bessie's absence, no valuable existence, while the aunt's dim corner seemed to glow, for the first time, with a quiet vitality.

"I expected, you know," after greeting him she surprisingly began, "that you would come to-day; not, of course, that I have stayed away to receive you. It is many years now since Lady Rolleway last invited me." He murmured on a note of sympathy as she continued, "You must find this, I am afraid, after your upbringing a very quiet neighbourhood. Indeed there has never been much amusement here for young people. When my brothers and I first used to go about the Hills had evening parties sometimes at South Bruton, not six miles from here, and people from London often staying there. But our father was in some ways what you would now call an old-fashioned man. Party or no party, all his doors and windows must be bolted at 10 o'clock, so that we saw little of the merriment. When he died I was to go to a little house he left me in London that was my mother's, but my brother lost his wife in the same month, and so I have always stayed on here for the children. But you are quite right" – Horsley had not spoken – "It is very dull in Burbridge. James and Bessie were not clever or ambitious as children, and I am glad to feel they have not missed what I could never have given them. They seem, really, not to resent the dullness. But you,

who have had everything – more, perhaps, than leaves you free to
guess how much an old woman can envy you – you must find all
this insufferable." She waved a thin hand to demonstrate the
furnished, meaningless room, and the town beyond its walls.

"But nowhere, I assure you," his loyalty to the absent Bessie
drew from him, "could so small a town shew more hospitality than
I have already enjoyed."

"No, no, no!" she interrupted him, "there is no hospitality in it:
you are only too polite to be yet aware of the dullness with which
we all gape at one another. I, believe me, would offer you better
cheer, but you can see for yourself the bareness of my poor
cupboard. If I had only my little London house, and, do you know,
I have never seen it – I might entertain you on your proper footing.
But I have begun to feel now that the days for gaiety have, perhaps,
all slipped past me. I believe if I found myself in London I should
not know what to do first."

"There would be a great deal," assented Bracton politely. He
had not been taught, poor youth, to be gay, and had he not learned
to be well-mannered, must have been shocked a little by the frail
old lady's abruptness. He turned the conversation with tact to a
recent royal marriage, rumour of which must have sounded, he
judged, even in her quiet corner, and, in a short time, took his leave.
But his curiosity, that appetite for the unknown with which even
the best regulated young man must, sometimes, feel enhungered,
was stimulated by that glimpse of the "Ant" in so unforeseen, so
improper an aspect. The discovery that she did not draw back in
horror from James' and Bessie's fastness, but had grown weary,
rather, was impatient even of their slowness, shewed him a subject
matter – he was himself now growing bored in Burbridge – for
research; and, as the summer waxed and waned through a bright
succession of flowers in the Manticross borders and of frocks upon
its lawns, he found several occasions to slip, expressing regret at an
absence of James and Bessie on which he had, every time, before-
hand counted, into the old lady's company. I dare not say that a

conspiracy was hatched between them, but by summer's end, they were agreed upon a plan; nothing less than that he, when shortly her tenant's lease should have expired, should occupy her little house in Half Crown Street, and prepare there to receive her: – for she would play truant after half a lifetime within the precincts of Manticross, and would fling herself into his experienced hands; and he should guide her through the perilous raptures of a London season. To do him justice, there was no vice in Horsley Bracton. If he at first, accepted, it was that he shunned the impoliteness. Besides, she had everything in order. Her ships were yare; and she would burn them. She had written, unknown to James, declining to renew the lease which would expire on Lady Day. Bracton, after a year well-spent in Burbridge, would demand and surely obtain a month's leave of absence to study his Uncle's London way of business; and, after a month in the untried paths of life, Miss Anna would, to borrow a phrase of Bessie's, have found her feet. So far had plans been fixed when, on a murky December afternoon. "Great news, my dear young man," she surprisingly called out to him "he – my tenant – died on Saturday." James, Horsley knew, was gone for some days to South Bruton where Sir Hay Hill was in an apogee of litigation over his mother's jointure. Bessie was, for the day at least, in London, settling the pattern of a brooch for her 'Friendly Girls' at Christmas. So with a sense of security the young and the old conspirators drew together. No compassion, no compunction, but a sensible excitement in anticipation disturbed the 'Ant's' tone as she went into detail. Her tenant was indeed dead. He had lived alone for some years, and an indifferent married daughter now inheriting had, (perhaps through ignorance – the possibility was stimulating – that any James or Bessie, anywhere in the world, existed) sent point-blank to their 'Ant' an offer to give up the house, with the Dentwood furniture that still mainly plenished it, as soon as both parties might find convenient. This party, didn't the young man see, found inconvenience only in delay. The Bank would easily – he had worked so well – grant him a holiday before Christmas and, for her part, what pure pleasure to get away from James's flat champagne and Bessie's heavy plum pudding and to dine zestfully with him, with Horsley Bracton, Dante dining with Virgil almost, at the Savoy or Carlton. She had noticed, in earlier seasons, their bills of Christmas fare, canvassed always afterwards in the Church Times, and now to partake of it – what a benediction upon her lifelong sacrifice. She had actually written as much to the dead man's daughter; oh, a letter that couldn't, she admitted, in the sad circumstances, go; but he must draft her another. As indeed, to do justice once again, he did; and then the trembling heads drew apart – and the old lady dismissed him with a clasp of that hand in which she confidently reposed her future happiness.

III.

During the next week and whilst he set his part of the banking house in order – for he saw with a growing distinctiveness that, after such an amazing elopement he could scarcely hope to cut any kind of figure again in the financial world of Burbridge – Horsley Bracton had no news of the Dentwoods. The old lady, he supposed, was waiting, but not – he could scarce expect it – in patience. By the eighth morning these uncertainties had told so upon his ciphering that, to end the suspense, he took his luncheon interval easily and set out for Manticross. But he had hardly started when Bessie Dentwood, rounding a corner on her bicycle, almost over-rode him. "Ant's dead!" she astonishingly flung down at him as she leaped from the saddle. "Last night. I've just been round telling Mrs Sawbridge and I'm going to the bank. She liked you rather, I think. We're having the funeral next Monday and James will want some money in the house." Horsley stared at her with an incredulity which grew in him as his senses took her large figure in. She was attired in a knitted jersey of orange silk stretched at its lower hem over a grass-green skirt of homespun: these, and her clear, grinning features quite reargued the grim tidings behind which, as he apprehended them there appeared to be such an infinitely great deal more latent. Was the old lady dead? Then how – when – why? Had James and Bessie killed her? Absurd, if you like, but didn't they then regret her? Could they, all these years have spared her to the life she had died desiring. If so it was indeed a tragedy: an incongruity to which Miss Bessie's fantastic array ("After father died, we agreed we wouldn't ever put on mourning for 'Ant,'" she explained,) did base justice.

Horsley Bracton's politeness, which the Dentwood family seemed fated to exploit, came again to his rescue. Blending with the conventional phrase of sympathy an offer of assistance he turned and accompanied Bessie to the Bank.

Some of the great deal, there was latent, he learned at the funeral from James. Encouraged by a fortuitous absence one day of both her relatives Miss Anna had put on the outdoor clothes they let her wear, if the weather served, at their lawn tennis parties in summer, and had made her way first to the railway and so to London. She had visited, James went on, "a small house I have there: I let it, having no need of a London residence, many years ago: but, by an odd coincidence, my tenant died not a fortnight before 'Ant' herself. She must have got wind of this in some way, though it actually hadn't reached me then; but why she should have felt bound to go to London, when she hasn't set foot outside my house and garden these past twenty years—" James broke into a silence eloquent of his inability to judge his aunt's character, and, as the mourners wagged their heads reciprocally he took up his tale again with "But how she got to London and what else she did there; for she left Half Crown Street before three, the servants there tell me, and she didn't come back till the 'six-fifty; – well, God knows, I suppose."

Horsley Bracton turned homewards from the cemetery in acute discomfort, and more in sympathy with his friend, now he had heard her last adventure, than he had been able to feel in those summer days when she had so unnaturally outrun all his own simple ambitions. But there was more still to become patent; while James was preparing her modest testament, signed and sealed in his father's time, for Probate, there came to Burbridge a comment on those unaccountable London hours, in the form of another, beyond doubt her Last Will and Testament, signed and sealed almost in the article of death at a respectable London office to which the Half Crown Street lady had been enabled, perhaps, by her own recent experience, to direct her. By this act the Half Crown Street house, fortified by the savings of a lifetime during which she had made her economies, were bequeathed to "Mr Horsley Bracton in gratitude for the services he has rendered me whose importance he may never be able to apprehend."

IV.

What – James in his blunt way was curious – were these strange services? Bracton could not explain, and would have summarily declined the inheritance; but James, who dreaded scandals suggesting – were the will set aside – that the aunt who had been, by two generations, almost entertained in Burbridge society, was even potentially insane; with his legal formality of mind and his reluctance to shew disappointment or to suggest that he might happily have found some use for a little house in London, James forced the well-mannered hand: and Horsley Bracton is now a house-holder in the Parish of Saint George's Hanover Square, with a little competence that goes to pay his rates and taxes.

Though he has been long – and without scandal or necessity – removed from Burbridge and prosperous now in an equally remote provincial centre, his good manners are still in part at the Dentwood's disposal. For, annually, at Easter, he takes a fortnight's leave of absence in London – and there, living in Miss Anna's little house and drawing cheques upon her little legacy, he consecrates twelve days and nights (reserving the Sunday's only for his own soul's benefit) to the poor old lady's memory, in a round of well intended and exhausting but perfectly innocuous dissipation.

Published in The New Witness, December 12th 1919

TWO TALES

"Free Verse"

Venetia Bancok was so widely, not to say well connected that her first volume, *Coloured Waters*, had a circulation which the reviewers had not foreseen and were unable to prevent; moreover, with as many of these as could be identified she had taken the precaution of inviting them quietly to tea, first, in her own "rather charming" flat. Her parents, who were dead, had been the prodigal son and daughter, respectively, of two very creditable families, each of which, feeling that it owed a debt of honour to the other, was always ready with a kind word, and often with a more edible form of hospitality, her father's relatives for poor Caroline's children, her mother's for poor Henry's.

The kindest intentions do not, however, ordinarily soften creditable hearts to the purchase of even a "slim" volume, but at a time when the six-shilling novelist showed signs of regarding the Treasury note as the sole negotiable form of currency, three-and-sixpence, even for no more than four-and-twenty pages, was literally nothing; besides, the less there was to read in a book, sometimes, the better; so that, within a year, the five hundred copies for which Venetia had paid an enterprising publisher to pay an indifferent printer (who supplied the paper) had almost all made their way to the drawing-room tables of the friends of her generous and uncritical cousins.

Still, there is a limit; and this had apparently been reached precisely at the date on which Venetia's *Pale Rainbows* made its confident appearance. Most of her relatives, when she met them in shops or at restaurants, would confess to having seen the new poems; many were good enough to congratulate her upon her industry. But only Mrs Montresor, who had married into Bayswater and could afford to be lavish, had promised to buy a copy, and even that promise was uttered principally in the hope of extorting from Venetia's own lips the solution of a problem that had long vexed her kinswoman's well-nourished mind: "When people write books, Venetia – I've always wanted to know – do they have to write down every word that comes in the book? I'm sure I should never have the time."

But one purchaser, however gratifying it may be to meet her face to face, does not always make a "Second Impression," and Venetia's anxieties were in no way allayed when the remainder season began to loom upon her horizon. As a last resort she determined to consult her brother.

Justinian Bancock was an indeterminate young man of whom perhaps the nicest thing that had been said by his contemporaries was that, at any rate, he could not be living by his wits. By what on earth else live (their parents had left not a brass farthing between them) even his sister had never learned; it appeared to be something that was perpetually about to involve him in the obligation to go abroad with "a fellow he knew," but as she had seen him, a few nights ago only, at the Ballet it was with a fair certainty of his being at least in London, and a hope that his occupation would not be such as must screen him from his sister's gaze that she presented herself at his "residential chambers" shortly before luncheon, on a Friday in November.

The weather was inclement, and her brother from home. Venetia waited. His sitting-room had a social rather than a literary air; yet it contained two familiar volumes – her own, which she moved into slightly greater prominence, lest any other visitor should arrive – and a third, in manuscript, in which, as it lay open upon the table, she was startled to recognise the familiar profiles of "free verse." Verse fully as free, a momentary glance assured her, as anything of her own (about which there was not, of course, the least suspicion of "moral" disarmament) with a more daring incoherence of meaning than she had ever attempted, "cadences" in plenty, and an attractive use of alliteration. Justinian had been letting himself go with a vengeance. The poem that lay exposed to her curiosity began with a couplet that strangely moved its reader:

> The page gapes:
> Apes' paws pass apace

This was stronger, her generous soul admitted, than anything in *Pale Rainbows*, stronger even than the first roseate flush of *Coloured Waters*; what freedom, what cadence, what "significant form"!

But it was time for luncheon. Venetia slipped the book into the large black silk bag which she kept for carrying poetry in, and left. That evening her family solicitor (the one heirloom she had definitely inherited) telephoned to her. Justinian, it appeared, had now gone irreducibly abroad, though not so much with "a fellow he knew" as to escape from the fellows who claimed to know him, and his address would not, for the present, be made public . . .

The appearance of *Monks and Mannequins*, by Justinian Bancock, caused an appreciable stir in an otherwise dull publishing season. What is known to journalists as "space" was allotted to it, among "New Books and Reprints," in *The Times Literary Supplement* (which gave the exact dimensions of the book and the numbers of its pages), while a "critic" in one of the Sunday newspapers was understood to have said that it would recall *Piers Plowman*, the published comparison to *Piers Gynt,* being due, one assumed, to a compositor's error. Two firms produced pirated editions simultaneously in cities as far apart as Seattle (Wash.) and Boston, and it was against one of these that the Kwikrite Shorthand Inc. – a name new to Venetia – won the first of those actions which laid waste for ever the claim that she had so hopefully staked for a family acre upon Mount Parnassus. The "Key" to their *Shorthand Exercises, Part I*, was strictly copyright, it appeared, in all countries signatory to the Berne Treaty, and Justinian's rendering of the exercises themselves (made some years earlier, when he was momentarily aspiring to a private secretaryship, and discovered and abandoned in the course of a hurried removal) had been, even though made without access to the key, perfectly correct, the only correct thing, indeed, that he could ever be remembered to have done.

Limited Editions

Louisa Pertalough was the only child of two comfortable and contented parents situated in the very heart of residential South Kensington, upon one of those great, horizoning thoroughfares along which young men may be observed to proceed, with the most honourable intentions, every Sunday afternoon. If, in other words, Louisa had stayed at home, going once a year under proper surveillance, to the exhibition of the Royal Academy, and dancing, when necessary, in the Empress Rooms, she might by now very possibly have been married, if not within the bounds of the Peerage (though these are always capable of expansion) at any rate some-where in the "Companionage, etc.," which forms so indispensible an adjunct to that volume.

But Louisa, fortunately for posterity, was of sterner stuff, the stuff which made Drake and Frobisher, Cœur-de-Lion and Disraeli (and through these men, England) what they were (and what England is); hers was the explorer's habit, the colonist's, the culti-vator's, the creator's; in a word, genius.

Beginning at an early age with a basketful of silkworms, a model handloom and a selection of Maypole soaps, she had throughout a whole London season dressed her dolls herself; after which, she felt, somehow, that she was too old for dolls. Later in life a fretsaw and a paintbox had helped her to produce quite a number of little wooden figures, many of which, if one looked at them not too critically, bore a distinct resemblance to one's favourite actor or actress in his or her latest London success. Several people had pronounced these figures to be "awfully clever," and one or two of them had actually found purchasers at a charity bazaar to which

Louisa had sent a generous consignment. But after all, as she had heard it splendidly put in a friend's studio one evening by a tawny-bearded young lion of the Canning Town group, who had success-fully defied the crushing classicism of Whitechapel and were erecting an academy of their own, "there is something dreadfully sterile about mere creation." Hers was rather, Louisa felt, the mother's or the middleman's part; to present the created object to an applauding world.

It is probably on record, somewhere, who discovered or invented the art of printing, though it is not known why. It is demonstrable, however, that this art, which has brought pleasure to thousands and profit to not a few of our countrymen, has so greatly developed in England over the last four centuries as to be now, in the mature opinion of the Ministry of Health, "an indispensible element in our national existence." Caxton (who appears to have set up his press actually within the precincts of the Palace of Westminster, where for many years he supplies successive Chairmen of the Kitchen Committee daily during the Session with printed menus, copies of which are now extremely rare) used wooden type, while this story, should it ever see the light of publication, will most probably be cast in an amalgam of various base metals; Louisa's type – for it was in Caxton's tradition, rather than Drake's or Frobisher's, Cœur de Lion's or Disraeli's that she was impelled to follow – was of india-rubber.

She had read a good deal about typography, which was appar-ently what they called it, in a magazine called THE LONDON MERCURY which her aunt Lucy (who was frightfully clever, and had often sent in essays to *Books of To-day*, and indeed knew Mr Humphreys personally) used to bring home at the end of every month (but quite clean, really) from her club, the Lady Divers'. She was familiar, therefore, with such terms as "old face" (which was like the dreadful nickname some of them had had, at school, for the headmistress) and "serif" (which had something to do, she thought, with the runaway marriage that silly girl Isabel

Fumbridge had made at Edinburgh, with a naval officer, during the war), but she could never quite make out from the articles what they meant, and the plan of engraving her pages on copper plate seemed too difficult and expensive, besides needing acids, which her mother would never allow her to use. The toy counter at Gamlingay's was her foundry, and capable of supplying her with as much type as she was ever likely to require, at a shilling a box, including a pad and a little bottle of very sticky ink. The printing itself was great fun, though very difficult. You first of all "set up" the type with a pair of metal tweezers between parallel lines of metal on a wooden board like a hairbrush, then you had to go and wash your hands very carefully before touching the paper, of which you spread out as many sheets as would lie without overlapping on the schoolroom table. Then you inked the type and pressed it down tremendously hard upon the paper; and if you didn't move it at all you were alright, but if you did the sheet was spoiled, and had to be thrown away. After the first few months Louisa's hand learned to control the type with comparative certainty, and at least half of her printed pages were good enough to show visitors, and even to ask people to buy. She contented herself at first with quite short pieces, that could be done with one box of type; nice bits from Stevenson about courage when one was ill, and all that sort of thing, and some verses by an American poet called Whittier, that she had got as a prize at school (only this was a mistake; because it had been a quite different man, something Whitman, that she had heard them all talking about at the studio). Then the most wonderful thing happened; she received an order to print a book.

It was quite a short book, for there would only be eight pages, some with no printing on them, by Venetia Bancock, and it was to be called *Jades*. There were three poems in it; the first was about a Swedish governess, and it was lovely; the second – Louisa hardly liked to print the second, as it didn't seem quite nice, but Venetia assured her that it was all right, really, and was about a person who had said beastly things about her brother. (Justinian Bancock had been travelling for the last year, in Sicily, for his health, which had been dreadfully bad since quite early in the war.) The third poem was, of course, about Queen Victoria and was very bitter. Then there were to be two illustrations; these were copies of jade ornaments that Venetia had in her flat, and must be printed in green ink, so as to "lend" the book a "distinctive charm." This part seemed very difficult to Louisa, but she knew that two of Venetia's uncles had married "Honourables" and so she hardly liked to refuse. Only, there was no green ink in the house, and even if she got some she had never been any good at drawing, and if she copied the illustrations on to the printed sheets she would be sure to spoil half of them. She might, of course, do the illustrations first, and print the poetry afterwards, but that would mean wasting a great many too, and perhaps smudging all the illustrations when she pressed the type down. Venetia, who knew all about books, having published several already, told her that the illustrations would be printed upon the sheets, and would only be coloured by hand. This puzzled Louisa a great deal at first, because she did not know how anything could be printed except from type, and surely there was no type to be had like Venetia's jade ornaments; but the poetess took her to see a young man with a moustache and a cough, who smoked far too many cigarettes and lived somewhere behind Wardour Street that you went down steps to, and he promised to have what he called "the blocks" finished next week, and to send the sheets along to Louisa with the illustrations already printed. They would be dreadfully expensive, but Venetia was going to pay.

One thing was certain: now that she was taking orders to print books, Louisa must leave home. Not in any bad sense, of course; Louisa was a thoroughly "nice" girl, and she would still be at home for all her meals, and to sleep. But the schoolroom table at Brifrons Gardens was not large enough, really, to do books on, and the printer's ink did leave such horrid stains in the bathroom basin when she washed her hands. Besides, Venetia said she must have a "colophon" saying where the book was printed, and how many copies and all that; and "printed at South Kensington" would be ridiculous, Venetia said; too dreadfully "bourgeois." Louisa didn't at all like that word. It meant a particular kind of type, she knew; but she was sure it must mean something horrid as well about South Kensington people, and though her family was not as "good" as the Bancocks, still, her parents were perfect dears, and everyone knew that Venetia's used to run away with all sorts of people, and had always been meeting each other at railway stations abroad and having to make friends again because nobody else would speak to them. But she didn't repeat this out loud, and anyhow she quite agreed that she ought to set up her press somewhere where people were more likely to want good printing done.

II.

She was extraordinarily lucky, because she saw an advertisement in the paper appear that very day of a place which seemed just the thing, and she went at once and found it had been taken by a tobacconist, but she could have it for a week as his sub-tenant, until he moved in his stock. So she took it at once, out of the money that her godmother would be sure to send on her next birthday. It had romantic associations, too, for a printer, for it was directly behind the Caxton Hall, what they called a "lock-up shop"; and there was no basement because the district railway station was right underneath. So she could have a season ticket, and be at home for all her meals in a few minutes, by simply locking up the shop and asking the policeman to see that no one broke in while she was away. The name for the "business" was still a difficulty, but her old governess, Miss Tidmarsh, who was very well read, made a splendid suggestion, and so it was called "Go, Lyttel Boke."

The sheets duly arrived, with the illustration beautifully printed and coloured in green by the man with the cigarettes, on Saturday afternoon. There were twenty-five of them, Venetia having decided to have just that number in the first edition, and more printed a little later, when those were all sold. Monday was a Bank Holiday, and though she was eager to begin work, Louisa did not quite like to open "Go, Lyttel Boke" that day, because of the Trade Unionists. She had heard a great deal about them from the Vicar of South Kensington, who took in the *Morning Post* every day, and the *Times* only on Saturdays, because of the sermons, and she thought that if the printers did have a trade union, and knew that she was working on a Bank Holiday, they might come and attack her. But when she saw that the evening papers were being sold, she decided that the printers couldn't have a trade union, or at any rate wouldn't mind her printing on a Bank Holiday, and so she got the palourmaid to telephone to the Oratory for a cab, and drove, with the illustrated sheet and her boxes of type upon her knee, to the Caxton Hall, where she paid the driver and told him she would walk the rest of the way; because, for all she knew, he was a trade unionist himself, and would drive off and tell the others what she was doing.

I believe Dante says, somewhere, what happens to people who work on Bank Holidays; anyhow it happened to Louisa Pertalough. First of all, when she was trying to fit the key into the door, she dropped the parcel of illustrated sheets, and as it had been raining a good deal and they fell into a puddle, two of the twenty-five were quite spoiled. Then, when she got inside, the table was dusty, and that spoiled a third, because people would never buy a book that had dust marks on its pages. And then she upset the ink-bottle over four more, when she was spreading them out. But she decided that she would save up and buy all the spoiled copies herself. Venetia was selling them at four shillings each, so that even if she spoiled the whole lot it would only be five pounds, and Venetia had promised to give her ten shillings for printing them. She set up her type from a copy of the poems in Venetia's handwriting, which was not very clear, and began printing upon the spoiled sheets, just to see. Each sheet had to be folded across twice, so as to make eight pages; the first was the title page, and the second had just: "This edition is limited to twenty-five copies, numbered and signed of which this is No . . ." The third had the poem about the governess, and it ended on top of the fourth, where there was an illustration. The second poem was on page 5, and the other illustration on page 6, and the poem about Queen Victoria on page 7, and on the last page there was just:

> printed.at.the
> sign.of.the.go
> lyttel.boke.in.
> the.city.of.w
> estminster.on
> the.seventh.d
> ay.of.augus
> t.nineteen.
> hundred.and
> twenty.two
> exegi.mon
> umentum.a
> ere.per
> ennius.

Louisa was glad that she had the spoiled sheets to practice on, because she was able to correct several slips that she had not noticed at first, and she was quite sure that everything was all right before she printed the first good one. When she had done it and let it dry she looked at it proudly and, taking a pen, wrote in on page 2 after "this is No." the figure "I," and then her signature with a great flourish, "Louisa J. Pertalough." Suddenly she remembered that it was Venetia who ought to sign the copies, and she felt horribly afraid, because she was sure that Venetia would be angry. Then, as she was printing the next copy, she heard a rattling in the corner, and she was certain it must be a mouse. Louisa was a very brave girl, so she stooped down to look for the mouse, but the rattling only grew louder and

louder until the whole room shook, and she thought that the trade
unionists must have found out what she was doing and plotted to
blow her up. She was dreadfully afraid for a moment, but then the
rattling stopped, and she saw what a silly girl she had been. It was
only a train going into St. James's Park Station, and that reminded
her that it was time to go home to tea. But when she went back to
the table she found that the ink-bottle had upset again, and the ink
had soaked through all the sheets except the last two. She printed
one very carefully without a single accident, and wrapped up the
other in tissue paper; then she put them both away on a clean shelf
and locked up the shop and ran downstairs to the train.

Next morning she returned to "Go, Lyttel Boke," and printed
the last sheet, but being a strictly truthful girl put on the back "this
eight" instead of "the seventh." Besides, the seventh had been Bank
Holiday. Then she waited for Venetia to come.

Venetia was very angry when she saw all the spoiled sheets, and
only half pleased when Louisa offered to pay for them. She said
that the illustrations alone had cost more than five pounds, and
that people didn't publish poetry to make money, but so that the
world might enjoy beauty, and how could the world enjoy what
Louisa Pertalough kept in a drawer in South Kensington. When
she saw the copy which Louisa had signed by mistake, she turned
quite pale with anger and said that poetry was a vocation, whereas
printing was merely a trade, like reviewing; and how dared Louisa
sign her poems? Louisa was very sorry, of course, and quite fright-
ened and hardly ventured to tell Venetia what she had just noticed,
that she had printed one of the two "good" copies the wrong way
round so that the illustrations came in the wrong order. However,
Venetia didn't mind that a bit, only she said that as the copies were
different, and one was dated "this eighth day of August," it had
better be made into a second edition. So Louisa printed "Second
Edition" on the title-page, and Venetia went out to Victoria Street
and got a lovely box of chocolates tied up in silky blue string which
they threaded through each of the two copies to make it hold

together; and they put them in the window and then ate the chocolates while they waited for booklovers to arrive and buy them.

No one came at all for quite a long time; then three very young soldiers passed, from the Wellington Barracks, and stopped and looked in at the window; then they nudged one another with their canes, and one of them said something, and they all laughed and sauntered on. Then a woman-policeman came up and looked at *Jades* with a pained but dutiful look, as if she felt that it ought to be prosecuted. Then two rather stout gentlemen came out of the station, and they looked so friendly and nice that Louisa felt sure that they must be Mr Belloc and Mr Chesterton, who (she knew) spoke at meetings in the Caxton Hall. But she didn't say anything about them, because Venetia hated contemporary literature, and thought it "démodé." Presently Venetia had to go, and as it was getting late Louisa locked up the shop and went home to luncheon.

Her father scolded her a good deal before he would give her the money for the shop and to pay Venetia for the spoiled copies, but her mother comforted her by saying that they were all going to Bexhill-on-Sea next week, for a month, and that if she behaved well one of her aunts had almost decided to present her at Court next season. After that it was impossible for her to sell poems about Queen Victoria, especially with the Guards' barracks so very near. Luckily the tobacconist began to move in that afternoon, and when she paid him the week's rent he told her she had a rare head for business, which comforted her a good deal. But the first and second editions of *Jades* remain unsold.

Venetia Bancock says that Louisa is a "chit," whatever that means. She has taken to reciting her poems now, which ensures her a wider public.

Published in The London Mercury
Edited by J.C. Squire
Volume VIII
1923 May to October 1923

THE MOUSE IN THE DOVECOT

They had seemed, and not only to people who did not know them, so entirely happy with and in one another – "As I always say," was how Mrs Mangotsfield put it, "such a contented couple – and no children to bother them, like I've had!" – that the report of Archie St Columb's having left his wife caused a shock which was effaced only by the subsequent and precisely coincident shock of learning that Nell had, almost simultaneously, left her husband. They had travelled, as was possible from their station, to different London termini and were now interviewing, it might be assumed, their solicitors in the quietest corners of each of the public sitting rooms in the Paddington and Great Central Hotel's, each unavoidably within earshot of the other's lurking and obvious detective.

Nell St. Columb was so innocent a little pet of a woman, all white dimples and black velvet, a suffragette in her day, of course, and one who would not have stopped, it was hinted, at taking life, but now, safely enfranchised, never bothering to record her vote, the demurest hostess conceivable of what could just, with an easy stretch of courtesy, in letters or conversation, be referred to as a country house. Archie was by some dozen years her elder, a thin, almost withered man, not loquacious. In his youth he had shown promise in the more theoretical branches of sanitary engineering, but the intestacy of an aunt had made it unnecessary for him to – in Mrs Mangotsfield's expressive phrase – "soil his hands," by providing him with a home in one of the more accessible parts of Buckinghamshire, and with the means to indulge himself now and again in the publication of brief but pregnant essays on the Economics of the Future, one of which was well known to have drawn a significant comment from Mr Sidney Webb. Nell, alone of the pair, hankered still after London. The first years of her married life had been spent in a Bloomsbury lodging, and she still sighed, as she would engagingly tell her country neighbours, for the "smell of kipper on the stairs." Periodically she made a descent upon the Capital, and bought back with her always the report of some enchanting new discovery: a dramatist whose play had been on the very eve of acceptance by the famous manager just, unfortunately, deceased; an actor whose West-End engagement a similar misfortune had cancelled; a journalist simply teeming with ideas for a new weekly; a painter who had already revolutionised everything hitherto attempted in that branch of art; a girl who had for some years been planning to write the most devastating novel about a boarding-school in Scotland. As many of these as could be persuaded, as there were few who could not, would follow her into the country, where Archie, proud of his house and of his wife, was a scrupulous if unappreciative host; and Buckinghamshire had begun to see in The Roundel (for so it was named) the crystallisation of yet another brilliant in the coronet already glittering with the names of Penn and Hampton, Chesterton and Shorter, when the prosperity, the contentment, the very existence of this throbbing little nucleus were in a moment inexplicably shattered.

Inexplicably by the world; but there was little that Mrs Mangotsfield could not explain, if she gave her mind to it. Descended from the last Hereditary Steward of the Chiltern Hundreds, who had been deprived of his privileges, and of life itself, by the iniquitous King John, she had retained all the dignity and much of the authority of that historic office. She had not been present at the explosion; no, but the facts soon reached her. Quick to discern the inessential, the mere embroidery of the story, and able from the stillroom of her experience to supply what was lacking, she had the whole ready, and had put it in circulation before the reconciled St Columbs could return from what, they were anxious to have it supposed, had been no more than a shopping expedition.

In the course of her last raid on London, Nell had fallen in love with a perfectly adorable actor, Coultarte Legthorpe. Nearer forty now than thirty five, he had constantly been within sight of the

most brilliant and had always merited success, but his modesty had
kept him within range of a few lifelong friends, and his name had
gradually ceased to attract the attention of the critics. Still, "Mr
Legthorpe gave a praiseworthy rendering of Orsic," had figured,
under the headline "London Theatricals," in the *Scotsman's* comment
on a recent performance of *Hamlet* given, at one of the smaller
theatres, in aid of the Hostel for Feeble-Minded Mothers, and
Legthorpe was greatly in demand by the societies which seek to
relieve the dullness of London Sunday by special performances of
an interesting and sometimes intimate nature. In this field his efforts
had earned him more than one stinging tribute from Mr W. J.
Turner, which, with the rest he pasted carefully into a little book
bound in violet morocco.

To look at, he was most noticeably arms and legs, with a face
in which, over the hard features of Elizabeth Tudor, played the
enigmatic smile of Mary Stewart. (He had indeed, in his earlier life,
impersonated each of these ladies in provincial pageants.) His health,
which seldom varied, was a source of keen interest to him and of
much anxiety. He neither smoked nor drank, having a weak, though,
it must be added, an exceedingly warm heart.

On a previous visit, Nell St. Columb had met, at a London party,
Vivian Patonwell, a dramatist with the contempt for all actors which
only a partially successful dramatist is justified in feeling. Here was
another perfectly delightful man, who simply must come down to
the Roundel. And come, very shortly, both he and Legthorpe did,
inviting themselves, as ill luck would have it, for the same few days,
during which the house was already to be almost filled with a party
of economist friends of Archie's. Pantonwell was the first to arrive,
on the Friday, by a train which left him barely the time to dress,
by candle-light, for dinner. His hostess studied him eagerly, an
admirable first-night audience, turning to register every smile that
appeared on her husband's dry features. The table-talk had the
spasmodic brilliance of a first-night on which only one actor has
rehearsed his part – Nell, an untiring prompter, rushing eagerly

upon the stage to supply deficiencies. Even for economists the guest had an epigram, at which even the economists tittered. A female politician, of great fluency, had been speaking the day before. "seeing that the gods," was his comment, "denied her the power of thought, it seems unfortunate that they should have saddled her with the gift of speech." The laugh was general: Nell sighed for pencil and paper. "Oh, you lovely man!" she cried at him, leaning across the table with outstretched fan. Archie admired his wife's spirit, but felt an inclination to frown, which he loyally, but with difficulty repressed.

It was not, however, until the next day that his displeasure took solid form. Rain had fallen all morning, driving the economists into his study, where he almost began to question the sufficiency of economics as a life-sport. After luncheon Nell begged him to take Mr Patonwell for a longish walk. She herself had already had an interview with her guest in which, "Mr Patonwell," she had pleaded, "I hope you won't think us dreadfully rude if we ask you to change your room. You see, I never can remember how many bedrooms there are in this house, and we've got another woman coming. It's such a bore as she-" Nell was about to add "invited herself," but remembered that this was Patonwell's case also, "-is a sort of aunt of my husband's and as she's rather stout, we can't very well put her in the attic. At least it's not really an attic, you know," she tried to retrieve the dismal prospect, "it runs all along the top of the house, and you get a simply glorious view of the Chilterns. No, please don't bother to go up and pack. They'll move your things. I'm sure you want a walk." No dramatist cares to be turned out of his bedroom for an aunt, still less for a sort of aunt, and the Chilterns were scarcely, after all, the Caucasus, though their inhabitants, he thought bitterly as he trudged beside Archie St. Columb through the rain seemed little more civilised.

A walk of some three miles, mostly through long and wet grass, brought them to the Golf Club, though he played the game but seldom, felt bound, as having a stake in the country, to belong.

Taking shelter in the club house, he offered his guest refreshment, but was told by a pert steward that, under the by-laws no alcohol could be served to members who had not played on the links that day. Pointing to a group of apparent drinkers who completely encircled the fireplace, he had been told that these were the Committee. "Hard cases makes bad laws," came in ringing tones from Patonwell. One could hear the purr of the curtain rolling down upon the stage as the whole Committee turned, with a single motion, to glare at the speechless St. Columb.

When they returned to The Roundel, Legthorpe and the sort of aunt had arrived, and were at the tea-table. The latter was indeed grotesquely stout, with a good-humoured, bristling face which made every man who encountered her want instinctively to offer the loan of a razor. During the war she had several times been arrested on the assumption that she was a male person (and must therefore be an alien) in disguise. She war a large agate broach, and subscribed generously to a number of those liberal-minded societies with influential committees and few members which are formed to promote or to oppose various unimportant movements and do, on the whole, as little harm as good. Although a spinster, she maintained a keen interest in Birth Control and Divorce Law Reform, and was frequently found, during the oyster season, discussing these and kindred topics in a small eating-house in Great Turnstile with Mr Hanbox, the eminent agnostic solicitor. She maintained, however, a whole tribe of young people, mostly the children of improvident clerical cousins, and when surprise was expressed at her apparently grudging nothing to people who were, after all, not dependant upon her, she would thunder: "I grudge them nothing but their little lives." She had already taken a maternal fancy to Legthorpe and, to his embarrassment, had given him much potentially valuable advice on the way from the station to the house. Nothing more need be said of her now, except that, as Patonwell reached the table, she was helping herself to the last of a plateful of toasted scones. Patonwell was presented to her, and scowled as

Legthorpe's name, qualified by "the actor, you know," was murmured to him by Nell. "What are you doing here?" he asked menacingly, and, "Aren't you playing to-morrow?" "But to-morrow's Sunday," protested Legthorpe weakly. "Well, isn't that your great day? No, Good Friday, of course!" He had been dragged, a few Sundays earlier, to a performance, given in support of the Trevethin Committee, of Schnitzler's *Reigen,* in which Legthorpe had given a very lifelike impersonation of the Count.

Nell St. Columb, after ringing for more scones to be toasted, turned the conversation; but it was an unfortunate turn. "Oh, Mr Legthorpe," she began, "I hope you won't mind; but you see, this is such a tiny house; we've had to put you in the attic. Mr Patonwell will keep you company. It will be quite like the trenches," she ventured hopefully, to be cut short by Patonwell's "Very! . . . A cross section," he added, with a glare of open hostility. "I was never in the trenches," Legthorpe unnecessarily explained, touching his peccant heart. "But I played a great deal to wounded soldiers," he added apologetically. "We couldn't all be of military age," was the sort of aunt's drop of comfort. But Legthorpe was already happy; before leaving London he had heard, in the Green Room Club, of a scheme for the endowment of a Repertory Theatre at North Shields, and Repertory Theatres had kept him afloat in the past through much stormy weather. When the toasted scones had arrived and had been eaten, Nell broke up the party with, "I'm sure you'd all like to see your rooms," and lead out the sort of aunt. As they crossed the hall a telegram was given to Patonwell which told him that the production of his play, *The Two Cicely's,* must again be postponed, owing to the sudden illness of an actor. "Actors! They are always having sudden illnesses, curse them!" was his dark thought as she followed his host upstairs. The sight of the evening clothes which "they" had laid out on his bed did not improve matters. "Why couldn't they sleep in the attics?" he questioned, thinking of the row of comfortable servants' bedrooms of which he had caught a glimpse on his way back from the golf course.

"That sort of woman always pampers her servants. And lets her guests rip – to be shut up in an attic with an actor."

He came down to dinner in no better temper. The attic, which was some thirty feet long, was divided by a partition, which stopped short of the rooftree, so that he and Legthorpe were compelled to overlook one another. Across this fence the actor had inadvertently addressed him as Pentoville, a misnomer which he had ceased to find amusing in his first week at preparatory school. Over the soup and fish he sat silent, until, catching Legthorpe's eye across the table, he asked icily, "Let me see; isn't Drinkwater writing a play for you?" Legthorpe blushed. "Oh, well nothing's settled yet." "What is it to be? *Little Bo Peep*, I suppose." "I'm sure that would be very interesting;" Legthorpe swallowed the insult. "I rather like sheep; don't you?" he turned to the sort of aunt for corroboration. "We all like sheep!" she boomed. An Anglican in her childhood, she still remembered several of the formulæ of public worship. "The sheep has been the curse of man," announced a Scottish economist of reactionary tendency, and embarked on a detailed account of the Highland Clearances.

Bed-time came as a general relief after an hour of bridge in which Nell several times revoked and her husband played in defiance of every economic theory. The latter was supplied by his sort of aunt, who proved, to his intense discomfort, that if he were to settle half his capital upon Nell and then allow her to divorce him, they might remain together without the necessity of paying supertax. Taking a scoring-pencil, she tabulated upon the ace of diamonds, the consequent effect upon the incomes of from three to fifteen pounds, and was still to be heard muttering stratagems by which a divorce might be secured when Patonwell and Legthorpe, each with a lighted candle, climbed the narrow stair to their attic. "A storm is brewing in the Chiltern Hills," the dramatist quoted, planting his candlestick on the dressing-table. "I hope not," came a bleat across the partition. "I'm terribly afraid of thunder." "You'd better make sure the sheets aren't damp," he was warned, and, at once panic-stricken, proceeded to thrust his hand between them. "I believe they are and I shall get rheumatic fever. Oh, why did I ever leave my home?" "I can't imagine," retorted Patonwell, and then, annoyed by the other's fluttering movements, "Better put a mirror in the bed and see." Excellent advice, but the mirror in Legthorpe's room was fastened to the wall, and in the other was an immense pierglass with frame and legs which had apparently been constructed in the attic, as no human agency could have forced it through the door. The actor continued to flutter. "I expect you'll find one downstairs," said his companion, now exasperated. "I saw one on the table in the drawing room." With an impulsive "Thank you," of relief and hope, Legthorpe in pink flannel pyjamas and a sky-blue dressing gown took up his candle and disappeared.

He reached the drawing room without misadventure, save from a moth which blundered into and extinguished his candle. A faint moonlight glimmered in the windows, and after much stumbling over an incredible quantity of furniture he reached and grasped a square foot of glass in a heavy frame. Thrusting it under his arm, he made his way back, but was intercepted on the first landing by Archie St. Columb. "Hallo, is anything the matter?" he inquired dryly, identifying the invader with an electric torch. "No thank you," Legthorpe hesitated at the incivility of explaining to his host the cause of his alarm. "It's only something I left downstairs. I wanted it. I couldn't sleep without it," he added lamely, as the glass slipped from his arm and fell. St. Columb's torch swept the floor. Between them lay an immense photograph, framed in silver, of a little woman in evening dress, all white dimples and black velvet, with the sprawling signature, "Ever your own most loving Nell."

Published in the London Mercury, August 1923.

WAR SERIALS

HALLOWE'EN

I.

There is no doubt the battalion had grown thoroughly sick of it. After opening the ball near Mons, two months ago, they had just had enough time off to squirm round sideways from the Aisne to this La Bassée country, than which – even in their Lanarkshire or Lancashire homes – few could remember an unlovelier; and the La Basseé adventure had not, so far, been very successful.

"D" Company had come out of the firing line on the 27th and slept, or "stood to," in a pair of ditches by the roadside, and awoke to perform such fatigues as their limited cover allowed, and to dodge some very large shells in the performance, and to return before midday to their support line, where they consumed what rations they had, and thought hopefully of the Peace that Someone was to conclude before Christmas. And all day long a friendly battery (dissimulating its friendship) barked at them from very close in their rear, and shook down over them the remaining leaves from the roadside trees. And it began to freeze: and night fell. Then the rumour came.

No-one, you may have noticed, will admit to a belief in rumours, but everyone does what he can to help them on their way; and this one, despite their isolation in small groups and under shell-fire, passed rapidly through all ranks of the company till it found the three officers, sitting on some very wet straw about four feet below the road level, under a roof of brushwood, and eating peppermints.

"I say, we're going to be relieved to-morrow."

The obvious retort is censored. In one syllable it summarised the well-known facts, that every man in all the six divisions was fighting somewhere, and that the seventh had come out and gone up to Belgium, where they were holding their own against God alone knew what odds. The cavalry were round there, somewhere, also. "The Russians," who had figured largely in all letters home last month, had disappeared, torpedoed in the Channel, perhaps; anyway, France knew them not. So the rumour was sniffed at. But it was very cold, and everything had frozen now, except the straw and water we were sitting in; so rumour was something to go to sleep on, and we were glad of it.

Next day we got it from the Adjutant, and things looked brighter. Allison broke into the cottages and returned with an earthenware pot and an armful of chrysanthemums, which the frost had over-looked, somehow, in a back garden: these brightened up the home. The Captain's servant, with a more practical mind, found a hen, and an iron pot in which, having died quietly, she was warmed into a sort of edibility. And we finished the peppermints, and speculated about the future.

"We're going back for a fortnight's rest," said the Captain, "some-where behind Calais."

"The War may be over by then," put in Bob who was writing home.

Allison, who had joined up four days ago, after a prolonged diet of soles, at Saint-Nazaire, was most full of *joie de vivre.* "I know, we'll have a Hallowe'en party – it'll amuse the men – and duck for apples.

"There are plenty of apples" – Bob teemed with general knowl-edge – "in the north of France."

"There's plenty of water," said the Captain, with the little snarl of a laugh that he used to frighten us into action in emergencies.

Allison dwelt on his plan lovingly, and had almost got the Captain's consent to it, when an orderly's head appeared in the doorway. He had brought a push-bike for Allison and a written order to proceed on it to the Regimental Transport, where he should leave it and proceed on foot to Brigade Headquarters, as guide to the advance party of the somethingth-or-other Gurkha Rifles, who would relive the Duke of Rothesay's Light Infantry on the night of the 29th–30th.

The frost had slipped away unnoticed in the darkness, and a heavy rain was falling. Allison wore a Burberry over his greatcoat, and, on his Sam Browne belt, a revolver, fifty cartridges, field-glasses, a prismatic compass, a waterbottle, a haversack, and (mark you) a sword. It is difficult to believe it, but in those archaic days, and even on push-bikes, people did wear swords, and with this bumping against him or sticking between the spokes of his back wheel, Allison paddled out along the dark and quite unknown road. . . and ran bump into a little gesticulating knot of Indians, and recoiled into a shell hole. It was not a very deep one, luckily, and the Gurkhas baled him out without difficulty.

II.

So the great relief began. And so, that night, but not without delays and difficulties, the Duke of Rothesay's got away for their holiday. For some reason each battalion had permission to move on completion of relief; and five battalions moving simultaneously, in file, along the same road, on a wet night in October, in companies or platoons, at irregular distances, within earshot of the enemy and under spasmodic shell-fire hardly went with the regularity and precision of a ceremonial parade.

However, by six on the morning of the 30th, we had got well away from it, and into a hamlet where the Quartermaster met us with a lantern and a list of billets. "D" Company were packed neatly into two small farms, and our three officers were sitting on chairs, over a table, with a stove burning and a feather mattress on the floor beside it, and had begun to bargain – all talking at once in various dialects – with two frightened-looking, sandy-haired young women – and their cousin, a veteran of *soixante-dix*.

There were five eggs in the house: we got those, and milk, and bread, possibly butter, and the inevitable canteen of tea may have been forthcoming, when the door was pushed open, and the

Captain's servant staggered in upon us, with a bulky and quite unexpected mail.

Now a parcels post at six on a winter morning would be considered a luxury in the best-appointed household. In our circumstances a mail, and such a mail, could only be called miraculous. There were sausages, the kind you can eat raw and in their skins, biscuits – chocolate – cheese, and I am not sure that there wasn't – a great rarity in those days – a bottle of whiskey.

At six we had been preparing for supper. By ten we had finished breakfast, had caught and bought two fowls for dinner, and, while the Captain and Bob shared the mattress, Allison, curled round the stove upon the tiled floor, consoled himself with the hope that the draught between front and back doors would at least dry his clothes upon him while he slept, and looked forward with a sleepy confidence, to his Hallowe'en party on the morrow.

By two we were up again and had washed ourselves – we had dined upon one fowl (the other was destined to a higher end, for, simmering on a stove in a very tidy kitchen when we evacuated Messen, she is, for all I know, simmering there, uneaten, to this day) – and had fallen in outside our farms and marched off over a long series of zig-zagging by-roads to the dirty little industrial town of M—, whose full name shall not sully these pages.

There we lay in a tile factory, and were glad, after a long march, to be there; but, for holiday-makers it was a queer thing that we didn't seem to have got any farther from the enemy.

Still, we slept.

Published in The New Witness, October 26th, 1916

III.

And we had a rude awakening. At about 1.30 the Adjutant flashed a light on us. We were to move off at seven, in motor 'buses, destinations unknown. And at seven, in some kind of order, we got clear of the town, embarked, and 'bussed off North, "D" Company leading, towards Belgium.

And now a second miracle happened whose chief effect was to preclude this story from containing anything likely to interest or excite the reader. For into the good town of Bailleul, and past the frontier posts, and up into Nieuwkerke "D" Company headed the column, or followed rather, close upon a reputed Rolls-Royce in which our C.O. was being wafted by the staff. "A," "B" and "C", and another battalion of our brigade followed. But at Nieuwkerke the Rolls-Royce disappeared and "D" Company's 'busses, our three selves and the Adjutant on the first of them, dashed off half-left on a non-stop run of three miles, and had all but got in touch with the enemy when they were rounded up by some swifter messenger on the nasty side of Kemmel Hill, and turned about to take their place in the rear of the Battalion.

So "D" Company went up there as the Battalion reserve. We got off our 'busses at or near the St. Quentin *cabaret* and fell in on the right of the road and wondered what in God's name was coming to us next. For, mind you, we were on holiday.

We may have marched a mile when a large shell falling pat on the left (our right) of the road, about ten seconds after the head of the column had halted about ten yards short of it turned Allison's doubts into a certainty that something very untimely was up, and that his Hallowe'en could not be spent in ducking, at any rate for apples.

There was a meadow by the road-side on our right, where a Cavalry Brigade had made some horse lines. Into this we disengaged and there got our orders. The Duke of Rothesay's Light Infantry would advance upon Messen and occupy it. Great coats and all superfluous kit would be dumped in the meadow to be brought forward later by our victorious transport. And so our second fowl was, for the time, abandoned. "A" "B" and "C" strode forward to the attack: "D" were condemned to hang about in the ditch or carry

up ammunition; to advance slowly as the day wore on, and to
wonder again and all the time what, in God's name was in store
for us.

We were, all three, well enough educated, but none of us had
ever heard of Messen. Nor, indeed, is the town commonly known
by that, its Flemish name; but the French word was so widely
canvassed, on another account, in the November newspapers, that
modesty keeps my pen from framing it, even now. It was a very
small town. A Cavalry Brigade had gone through it a fortnight
earlier and was entrenched in front of it to meet an overwhelming
force of the enemy, who had pressed them back into part of the
town on the 30th, when we and that other Battalion, the only free
lances, it seemed, in the British Army, were hurridly sent for. We
had to go down hill from where the shell burst, to cross the Steene-
beck by the road, then spread out to the right (as that other Battalion
was doing to the left) and up the corresponding slope, invitingly
tricked out with bursting shells, and over the skyline – and then?
. . . Our three "D" Company officers gathered behind a little hut
halfway down the slope, and polished up their field-glasses; and
wondered what had made them leave, in the field with their great
coats, two loaves of bread and what remained of yesterday's parcels.
Near the top of the opposite slope a windmill stared blankly at
them, and seemed at frequent intervals to eject spent bullets very
pointedly at Allison's head. Just over the hilltop peered the roof of
a great rectangular church tower. To the right was a *cabaret (Au Bon
Fermier)* and a street of cottages that straggled from it over the hill
into the unknown. And among these things our first three compan-
ies moved steadily forwards, our shells and the enemy's bursting
impartially among them. We felt very hungry.

About four o'clock we moved on. Nothing very much happened.
It was quite dry and had begun to freeze again, and we were still
very hungry. Past the *Bon Fermier* we slipped up the straggling street
and into what there was left of a town beyond it. This was shelled
and dismantles and fatuously barricaded at the corners. Parties of

German prisoners passed us under escort and disappeared into the dusk we had come out of. A rumour filtered back that "B" Company were in the heart of the town, cheek by jowl with the enemy, and that G— had been killed. The machine-gun officer appeared, and in a melancholy voice (he had seen a lot of fighting) suggested "This is about the end of the Duke of Rothesay's"

"Oh, well," said Allison "there's the 2nd Battalion in India still, and the 3rd at home, and then there's these new Armies somewhere."

But the general opinion was that they and that other Battalion would end up here and that for two Battalions battered out of existence at Le Cateau, and at the Aisne again and round La Bassée, such an end would be quite fitting. Nobody was really discontented . . . And at home, I daresay, they had begun to duck for apples.

At Messen, meanwhile, the frost was keen. Bob had found a tin of bully somewhere, and Allison half a loaf of bread in his haversack, which they divided. A young goat wandered down the street (towards Calais) very nonchalantly, as if there were no war on. By the grace of God she was a female, and Bob milked her into the empty bully-tin. A cavalry subaltern appeared, relieved, I suppose, by one of our other companies, and complaining of hunger. They'd been in the trenches here for ten days and without rations for the last two.

"I've only got this crust, I'm afraid," said Allison, who was still tainted with *joie de vivre*.

The cavalry subaltern took it without a word, and walked off into the darkness, chewing.

At last we got into the town, disposed ourselves along the main street by the tram-line, and lay down on the frozen pavement to await the morrow. Now, two nights ago, the Gurkhas had relieved us in thick darkness, but to-night, as on those first weird nights of mobilization there was a moon up of "extraordinary splendour and beauty." The street ran down hill to the right with a shimmer of tram-lines into the unknown; facing us were the church tower and the walls and two great gates of a convent school. This had been shelled incessantly and had burned, we were told, for five days; it was a tangle of ruins. In one gateway lay an iron bedstead, abandoned in the first evacuation, and since tormented by fire.

Allison was detailed to take charge of the convent and all it contained; to see that there were no Germans alive inside it, and to post sentries at all gates and breaches in the wall. He could use a platoon.

He went round alone first, and spent two hours exploring the precints: moonstruck with the blueness and the glamour and the ruin, stagestruck too, a little, at this his first full dress appearance on the field of battle. The great church was roofless and empty, and from its walls came pittering constantly dust and plaster. The lead of the windows, loosened by explosions, rattled furtively and at strangely regular intervals: as though some power of evil were at work up there, filing the bars of the sanctuary.

He went down at length to the lower quadrangle, and almost fell into a dead cow that lay there, swollen into a grotesque feather bed in the moonlight. In the garden he found a sow in like case. He came down to the wall and listened. There was no shell fire now from either side, no musketry even: but near by and farther and as far as he could hear on the frozen field wounded men were groaning.

As the moon glared down on him he felt himself an untutored young actor moving awkwardly behind the scenery and dazed by the limelight – with all the action of the stage going on a yard away: they hadn't reached his part yet: he might recognise his cue when it came. . . And then, suddenly, he got it. Two yards of the wall had been crumpled in by a shell, and under the ruin lay a ladder. A cavalry subaltern, who had been observing from the ladder, lay still and smiling, his right hand still clenched on his revolver. Beside him, dead also, was a sergeant. Allison stepped through the broken wall, and was at once upon the stage. In the fierce moonlight he felt enormous, and visible a mile off: but no one seemed awake now except the wounded, who groaned continuously, close at hand, farther and afar off, and the stretcher parties who were taking them by degrees and very noisily back to safety. He walked on to a contested spot where many had died on either side; each in the little pit made with his entrenching tool, waxen in the moonlight they recalled irresistibly the waxen Marat, dead in his bath, at Tussaud's. Allison passed on, by a sort of moat to the bridge across it which took him in by the South gate of his Convent. He collected the platoon allotted him, and placed sentries at the gates and gaps in the wall. There were no Germans inside, he could assure them. This officer must be identified, when daylight came, and buried. For the platoon sergeant he had found a handy little weigh-house inside the South gate. He must apologise for the broken window glass, which littered the floor. There was some straw, on the other hand.

His self confidence revived: he went back into the street to find the Captain, who was stamping up and down cursing and threatening to shoot the men who had put straw over their feet, and then chuckling at his own ferocity.. In the end the frost prevailed, and a straw rick being found, as by a miracle, in someone's back garden, all ranks resorted to it for what bedding it might supply. Some curious point of honour prevented "D" Company from taking any shelter that night. Two of the fighting Companies were in houses, and did well enough; the reserve lay on a stoney pavement outside the open doors of a most comfortable little street of dwelling houses and awaited the morrow. Allison begged the Captain to come round his sentries. The Captain refused, being sleepy: yet it was barely two o'clock. Finally the three lay down on a wisp of straw, and lay awake there. The frost hardened. About three an orderly appeared from "C" Company, demanding Allison. "A beg your pardon, sir, but Master Davidson says, there a German sniper diggin' himsel' in on the roof o' the kirk, an' will ye please just come along an' see him for yourself." Remembering that the "kirk," though quite roofless, was in his province, Allison got up and followed; and came, outside the church, to four "Black Maria" holes about twenty feet across and ten deep and beautifully dressed by the right. Behind them was Lieutenant Davidson with a rifle. "Listen!"

Allison heard again what he had interpreted before as the tapping of the window leads against each other and said as much.

"I think," urged Davidson, his senior, "that it's someone digging himself in."

"He could only be protecting himself, up there, against our aeroplanes," answered Allison sagaciously "and even then it'ld be no protection. Fire your rifle at him."

Bang! There was an awful hush. Some plaster fell from the walls and the tapping steadily continued.

Allison went back to bed.

Published in The New Witness November 2nd, 1916

IV.

So Hallowe'en passed and All Saints Day began. By 6.30 some rations had come up, and Allison awoke to se the Captain standing over him, attempting to spread plum and apple jam with the point of a bayonet on a half loaf that, like the jam tin, was balanced on a window sill, about the level of his shoulder.

"Get up," snarled the Captain.

"That's just the worst of it," philosophised Allison: insubordinately perhaps, but the Captain was not really a Captain then, and the three of them met on upon a kind of equality. "I'm all right at night, but you're so infernally active in the morning.

"Owl!" answered the Captain.

V.

By 9.30, Allison was in his element. They had explored all the houses and found any amounts of cellars (in case of bombardment) and kitchens, and a piano, and a collection of picture postcards. He could also explore the convent by daylight. One gate proclaimed, in great letters of bronze, its foundation in such a year, by Maria Theresa, as a school for orphaned daughters of her Austrian soldiers: the lower gate spoke of its enlargement in such another year by the Belgian King, Leopold I. A great M and D of bronze, from one of the dates, he had picked up at his feet, and contemplated a moment as "souvenirs" but, more prudently, left them. Weight avoirdupois tells with a foot soldier.

The great coats had come up, also the day's rations, and the Captain's servant, ever more practical, had cajoled the second hen into a caldron of water, had got a fire lighted in someone's kitchen, and tea boiling. The men were stowed away underground, and Allison had found a rare cellar in the convent, not half full of potatoes, in which he had almost induced Headquarters to establish themselves when the order came. The Duke of Rothesay's Light Infantry would fight a rearguard action, while the Cavalry retired from the town.

Allison was to go first, with Sixteen Platoon. He might occupy the windmill. He made for it, but, a British shell getting there before him, in five seconds the mill was in flames. They spread out to the left and fell in with that other Battalion, not two hundred strong now, and compared notes. What had happened? No one quite knew; it was believed that there were some fresh troops of great promise further to the left, but that their promise was not wholly fulfilled: and so there was a hole in the line.

Being Sunday morning it was now about Mass time, and they looked curiously over towards Wytschaete Church, expecting conventionally to hear a ring of bells. Instead, the conical spire flickered up like a lighted candle: then the whole tower was ablaze. Over the place fitly called L'Enfer they could see Germans come tumbling in their thousands. A brass band was playing.

The Cavalry must get away first and Allison, grown savage now after a whack on the head from some passing projectile, drove the scattered troopers – they were calmly sitting here and there among his own Jocks – like sheep before him on to the road – where they fell in and duly disappeared.

And now we ourselves were neatly sandwiched: for our guns had begun to shell an outlying row of houses just behind us while the enemy plastered the town and the fields in front. But we got out somehow, and by midday were spread out in front of the Steenebeek, and digging ourselves in for dear life with our entrenching tools. There were some notable deeds that day; "Big Murray's," for instance, who, finding his Company-Sergeant-Major left behind and spouting blood from a wounded lung, carried him half a mile in his arms before he found the wheelbarrow in which he bore him triumphantly through our line to the Dressing Station. Then there was that Platoon which Allison had posted in the Convent. They stayed at their posts, in default of orders, until, in the afternoon, with about five thousand to one against them, their Sergeant brought them quietly out. A touch of humour also, when the kind-hearted Allison found fourteen newly-weaned young pigs with their jaded mother, shut up in a barn, and promptly opened the door.

The hungry creatures rushed, as one pig, into the farm kitchen where that other Battalion had just established its headquarters.

VI.

It froze again that evening, hard: and, having nothing much to do we made bivouacs out of the little straw screens kept, for some purpose, in the neighbouring tobacco-fields; and awaited our relief. It came at last, and by midnight the company was gathered into old Isidore Deschildre's farm at Nieuwkerke. I remember, there, his grotesque old night-capped head popping out of a window to greet us and contorted, at the sight of us, I don't know why, with laughter. We were his guests for four days, and, but for having to 'stand to' in the road at night to catch German motor patrols, and to sit out in the fields all day to avoid German shells, we fared well enough. On the 6th we marched up through Ypres to take our turn in the "First Battle" there. But that is another story.

Published in The New Witness: November 9th 1916
BRAMANTIP.

FIELD PUNISHMENT

This article is not an immediate sequel to that published in the last three weeks under the title "Hallowe'en." It has been written, ad hoc, to throw some light on a subject recently made popular by the criticisms of Mr Blatchford in the Sunday Chronicle, and by some recent "Comments of the Week" in this paper. – B.

I.

By the end of February, 1916, the Duke of Rothesay's had been for two months resting. They were in a very small village about four miles from the river Somme at a point as far below the town of Amiens. They did a little digging and some route-marching, and a very great deal of kit inspection; apart from which, all ranks were both good and happy. There was no cabaret in the village, so small was it, but a chaplain who lived with our Transport managed to arrange for beer, which arrived in barrels and was duly dispensed in the village school. Suddenly, at night, came orders to be ready to move: and in the morning, after hours of worry and speculation, we moved out, bound northward to relieve French troops who, themselves, were under orders for Verdun. Next day, after going fifteen miles against a blizzard, with the north wind in our faces all the length of an arrow-straight Route Nationale, we arrived in the considerable town of D—. Here we stayed three days, enjoying the pleasures of civilisation; a hotel, shops, *buvettes* as befitted our various ranks, while the C.O and his Company Commanders went up twenty miles to the firing line to study the disposition of our Allies' strength there, and arrange the forthcoming relief. On the third evening all ranks are warned to be in readiness, and, about 10.30 next morning we parade to march out. Now Allison (who is

O.C "A" Company) discovers that three of his men are missing. Officers, N.C.O.s and men, burdened with their full marching order, for billets have been evacuated, run to and fro in search of the absentees, with the sole object of getting them on parade in time to keep the Company unspotted in the Colonel's eyes, and the Regiment, *a fortiori,* in the Brigadier's. Meanwhile, time passes; the Company must be ready to move. Allison scrambles onto a very high horse, and picks his way down the congested street till he comes opposite to the Adjutant, who greets him from the doorstep of the Headquarters Billet.

"Morning: you all ready?" – He is said, this Adjutant, to have made fewer unnecessary remarks than any man on the Western Front.

"Morning," answers Allison. "Three men reported absent."

"Pity. Can't you find 'em?"

"We've been looking for about an hour: they're nowhere this end of the town. One's an old hand at it, I'm afraid."

Allison rides back and orders three men to hand over the absentee's equipment to the local Military Police, so that they shall not be liable to punishment for losing it by neglect. Then the Battalion marches off going ten miles through the light, half-frozen mud of a clear Spring day, to billet in a tumble-down village off the main road. Next day they have gone ten other miles, and have reached the place appointed as a home for the Regimental transport, when, the Battalion having "fallen out on the right," the Second in Command comes up the road to Allison.

"I say: you'll have to send an escort back for those three men of yours: they've been found in D— by the police. Better choose some men of might, and make them march back to the Transport now and get their tea there."

It has been a tiring day to march through heavyish mud, and all the ranks look forward to the approaching inactivity of the trenches. Allison feels loth to detail anyone for the long march down to D— and up again, and curses the three absentees for the trouble they are giving. He chooses the solidest Lance-Corporal he has, and two who did wonders, last Sunday, in the Regimental Boxing Finals at D—. One of them got five years, last September, by Field General Court-Martial, for boxing too freely when in liquor, with an N.C.O.; and is, therefore, still on probation under the Suspension of Punishment Order. He is now a model of good behaviour, and one of Allison's closest friends in the Company.

The escort falls in and moves off into the dusk, towards the Transport, and presently the Battalion falls in and moves off the other way under a railway embankment by which the order *Défense de Trotter, Même aux Cavaliers*, amuses the more polyglot among us; for "the perished linesman," someone observes, "knows a sight more than to *trot* into Arras, in his marching order *and* a tin helmet, even without being told not to."

So we get into the town at last, and billet, for what remains of the night, in some of its many cellars; and lie about until the evening of the next day, when once again, as seven months ago on the Somme, we relieve a Regiment of French Infantry on the Scarpe. Next day, again, the escort and prisoners rejoin us: what expedients they have used, what 'lifts' obtained on lorries or ambulances meant for other freights, need not here be considered. The escort have brought up the prisoners, and the summary of evidence against them, and the whole party now join their respective platoons in our long platoons in our long and very thinly-manned line.

(A platoon, it may be said here, should consist of some fifty men, but generally in the trenches, we have about half that number. They are told off in three or four sections of sic, for the purpose of trench warfare, and are on sentry-go singly, by day, for a tour of two hours each: by night, in response to cries of "Two and Fours on!" and so forth, they are mounted in pairs for one hour on and two hours off. The N.C.O.'s remaining, after all the groups of six are filled, do not themselves go on sentry, but take it in turns to patrol the Company's sector, supervise working parties, or go out with an officer on patrol, as may be appointed them.)

Next morning, one of our three absentees is slightly wounded, and disappears from his trench and from these pages: this is duly reported by buzzer as "A Co. Casualty Return. 12 NOON. 4/3/16 One o.r. wounded, A." Which is to say, "No officers, but one 'other ranks' wounded; by rifle fire in front-line trenches." Half an hour later comes the message: "O.C. 'A' Co. – C.O. will see prisoners to-day at 2.30 p.m. – Adjit. D.R.L.I." So, after dinner, Allison, his Sergt-Major, and the two remaining prisoners paddle down through deep channels of melted snow to Headquarters, which occupy a derelict, but undamaged factory, hard by the Lille Road.

II.

As Allison finished the formality of "seeing" his prisoners, the Adjutant appears in the doorway.

"Prisoners all seen, Sergeant-Major?"

"All seen, sir." The Regimental Sergeant Major salutes

The Adjutant withdraws, then, reappearing, calls "A Company."

Allison enters the presence and salutes. Outside, the Sergeant-Major intones: "Private McLuckie, escort. Company Sergeant Major Walters."

"Good morning, Allison," says the Colonel. A rainbow vision – to his muddy subordinates – of polished leather, he sits behind a table covered deep in the papers he brought up with him, the more important of this morning's signal messages, and the papers that he was unable to induce the French Commander to take away "on completion of relief" two nights ago.

"Good morning, sir," says Allison, sweetly, handing the Colonel an interesting specimen of "Army Book 152" in which the crimes and punishments of his company are recorded and "Two cases, sir."

"Yes." The Colonel examines the open page. "That old rascal, McLuckie, again."

"He's been running pretty straight the last six months, sir. If you would punish him yourself I should be very grateful."

"March him in, Sergeant-Major."

The Sergeant-Major who is standing outside in the passage, looks out to the yard. "Private McLuckie, sir."

The prisoner is marched in. The Colonel takes up a pencil and reads from the book – "'Private McLuckie.'"

"Forty-seven one nine, sir"

"'In the field, on the 29th of February; when on active service; one: absenting himself from parading with the company for the trenches, at 9.30 a.m., and remaining absent till apprehended by Military police, at 12.15 p.m. (two and three-quarter hours). Two: Drunk and creating a disturbance.' Company Sergeant-Major Walters."

"Sir, on the 28th instant" – the slip passes unnoticed save by Allison – "I warned the company, at tattoo roll-call, that they would parade for the trenches in the morning. This man was present, sir. At 9.30 on the morning of the 29th the company paraded outside their billet. He was then absent. I reported him to Captain Allison, who had a search made through the battalion billeting area; but he could not be found."

The Colonel glances at the book. "Documentary?"

Allison reads the evidence of the Military Police, who had found three men of the Duke of Rothesay's with two drivers of the Army Service Corps, quarrelling in an estaminet, about 12.15 p.m. They were drunk.

"What have you got to say?"

"Sir, I wis not drunk. Hearin' that my brother in the Army Service Corps, whom I had not seen for fifteen years, was in the toon, I took the liberty, sir, of leavin' my billet, sir, for to seek him. I had no intention to be absent—"

"Yes, yes," says the Colonel irritably. "You've met that brother for the first time every time the regiment had been in billets. Captain Allison?"

"This man, sir," Allison begins in honeyed tones, "has been with the company nearly eighteen months. He has not been before you since last August, at Blank-sur-Somme. He has never shown any inclination, sir, to avoid his duty in the trenches." He pauses, remembering a court martial six months ago, as a member of which he gave two men ten years each for a similar offence – but without the charge of drunkenness. In his left hand he conceals the man's conduct sheet (sheets, rather, for there is a second almost full) which he hopes the Colonel will not ask to see.

Published in The New Witness, November 23rd, 1916

III.

The Colonel thinks for a minute. He hates the fuss and publicity of a court martial as much as Allison, and doubts its efficacy (now that punishments are suspended) as a deterrent. It is about that man's sixth "drunk," he thinks, but he will not look at the conduct sheet. Finally, "An old soldier, like you, McLuckie," he begins, "ought to know a great deal better than to behave as you do. To absent yourself from parading for the trenches is equivalent to cowardice" – McLuckie adds half an inch to his stature – " and the penalty for cowardice you know. You have been constantly before me, and I have no excuse for not sending you to a field-general court martial. You say you were not drunk: the Military Police say you were. You have also set a very bad example to two young soldiers, and have given a great deal of trouble to Captain Allison and to everyone else. Next time this occurs" – McLuckie looks hopeful – "you will be severely dealt with. Twenty eight days' Field Punishment, Number One." He enters the award in the book and adds his name and rank and the date.

"Thank *you*, sir," mutters McLuckie hoarsely, and is marched out.

"Private Dowell" is announced by the Sergeant-Major.

This is a young hind from East Lothian, with a blameless countenance and only about seven months' service. He has one or two minor offences in his sheet, but has, hitherto, hardly even seen the Colonel, and trembles, standing before him, as he has never trembled in a "listening post." After a stern admonition he is given twenty-one days' Field Punishment, and retires

"That is all of 'A' Company," mutters Allison, over the Colonel's shoulder, to the Adjutant.

"Eh?" – the Colonel forgets nothing – "I thought you had a third man."

"He was wounded, sir, this morning."

"A bit of luck for him. Badly?"

"No, sir; hardly a blighty one."

"Well I won't keep you, Allison, as I know you're busy. I shall be round your way about five; we might look at some of those superfluous French listening-posts."

"Good morning, sir." Allison salutes and rejoins his Company Sergeant-Major in the courtyard. The prisoners have already gone up, unescorted, to their trench where, later, Allison, passing a suspended ground-sheet and whatever lies behind it, overhears a question and answer:

"What did he give ye, McLuckie?"

"Twenty-eight of the best, lad."

SEQUEL.

It is on record that my great-great grandfather, visiting Paris in the days of Louis Quinze, paid fourpence "to see a man broken on the wheel." What price should I, then, ask, for circulating through the British Press the narrative of "The Crucifixion of Private McLuckie"? And what of the boy Dowell, who so lately, on his eighteenth birthday, went proudly into Edinburgh, and strode up Cockburn Street to the recruiting office? *Luogo e in inferno detto Malebolge.* Is he bound by his middle and his ends to some limber-wheel, that revolves bumpily, at about three miles an hour, along a by-road in Artois, in eighteen inches of congealed mud? Not a bit of it. The first four days they spent in the fire trench. For the next six they were in support to another regiment, to whom the whole company, the innocent with the guilty, were fully guilty in carrying up incessant meals from their cookers somewhere back across the Scarpe; in the intervals they toiled at the restoration of a French redoubt, which "winter's rains and ruins" had left in considerable disrepair. Then, for six days in billets, they were shut up in a barn in the headquarters' farm, parading frequently under the gigantic Provost Sergeant for "work of national importance." In the next six days in trenches Dowell's term expired; and, going again into billets, where a Field Cashier happened, obligingly, to pause in his endless round, each of them and every other man in the company received ten francs and answered "ten francs, correct, sir," and signed the acquaintance-roll, for all the world as if nothing had happened.

And what of the third man? His wound was not "a blighty one," and he rejoined the company in April, to find that Allison was sent down the line with a decidedly blighty "Trench Fever"; C.S.M. Walters had been given a commission; and a rat had eaten the "Documentary Evidence" which alone remained against him . . . And six months later, from a Sunday paper sent out from home, which the priests had often warned him to avoid, he learned that what he had escaped was "the intolerable torture of crucifixion," for which let us hope he was duly grateful. *BRAMANTIP*

Published in The New Witness November 23rd 1916

REVEILLON

"We'll have that chorus again now, please. Are you all ready? Oh, come along, *please.*" The stage manager turned wearily on his performers, who had scattered, as amateurs will, to all corners of the large hotel drawing-room, and were swapping stories, trying on costumes, practicing make-up, mixing drinks – doing anything but attend to the rules of the game.

It was past eleven o'clock on Christamas Eve, 1915, in the Home for Convalescent Officers at Nice. Thawed out by the sunshine and gaiety of the Riviera, our little clique had devised and obtained authority for a grand Christmas entertainment, of a kind never seen before or since. As the year was 1915, revue was imperative; as none of us was convalescent enough to write a revue, we dug out the stale idea of pretending to begin one and then switching off into something else. Costumes for the chorus seemed a difficulty until we worked out our highest common factor in really striking suits of pyjamas; this suggested the ruse that a hospital convoy should arrive on the stage just as the assistant surgeon had explained to the relieved audience that the entire cast of our elaborately prepared revue had been "returned to duty" for misconduct. After this all was to go well. We had an operatic tenor (whose merits we never adequately acknowledged) who stage-managed us into a kind of sufficiency and himself right out of convalescence and almost to death's door the week after; we had a blameless "London Scottish" Subaltern, whose purple kilt was a joy and a confusion to all the gossips of Nice; and three real Scotsmen of the "Heavy Comic" kind, who satirised the operations (dimly apprehended there) of the Liquor Control Board in a dialogue wholly unintelligible to nine-tenths of the audience, and deeply deplored, I have no doubt, by the rest. That afternoon we had invaded the Old Town, and ransacked a theatrical costumier's with remarkable effect. The old

man in it was a Norman, still quite at sea after twenty or forty
years' residence on the Côte d'Azur; he found in the Scottish officers
some relishable link with Jeanne d'Arc, and soon filled a dress-basket
with the strangest collection of garments ever catalogued.

So we came to our dress rehearsal. The stage was now set up
in the dining-room, decked out with every convenience that Nature
or the artfulness of the R.A.M.C could provide. We had dresses
now, wigs, paints, whiskies and sodas. The order of the programme
had been written out by at least three different authorities, claiming
equal competence. And after dinner on Christmas Eve we rehearsed,
and rehearsed.

Everyone suddenly realised that the show was going to be too
appallingly bad for words, and longed for some excuse to get out
of it. One or two stole on to the terrace and calculated the chances
of a just sufficient sprained ankle if they dropped quietly over the
balustrade and in among the cherry-pie and mimosa bushes beneath.
Allison yawned, and looked again at the clock.

II.

The rehearsal ended at last. Allison buttered and wiped his painted
cheeks, arranged collar and tie, found his British Warm somewhere,
slipped out of doors and through the lower gate, and found himself
at the head of a long, clear stretch of road descending into Nice.
Far away on his right, near Antibes, it might be, a lonely dog was
barking. Another took up the call. Soon it seemed that all the dogs
in the world were aware of the tidings: again and again, on all sides
of him, from hill and valley, incessantly they bayed. He thought of
Simaetha's hoarse whisper: –

> *Thestuli, tai kunes ammin ana ptolin oruontai.*
> *a Theos en triodiosi: to chalkion os tachos ochei.*

And with the thought, from the railway beneath him as a train entered the tunnel on its way to Italy, a solemn bell clanged. The dogs brought back to him remembered plains, far off by Somme and Yser, where the Armies of two Christian Powers were greeting each other at that hour as meaninglessly with a constant barking of rifle-fire. No, there was nothing more in it. Wheezing and crashing, the last train from Cimiez swung round the corner behind him, and passed Queen Victoria's statue ; it overtook him and he climbed aboard.

The Cathedral Church of Saint Reparta escapes the casual tourist's notice, hidden away in the old town of Nice. On a mismaze of narrow streets the tall houses are set, like the toys of some orderly-minded child inside the lid of their box, represented on this side by the river embankment, from which one can go down among them by various flights of steps. It is not a very old, nor a very great, nor a very beautiful building. There are a great many plaster pillars, painted to resemble marble, and a brave display of cherubs and flowers, and so forth, in blue and gold beneath the ceiling. In front of it is a small "place," where every Sunday Monseigneur's small carriage and pair of horses, proportioned, it might seem, to the width of the surrounding streets, await his arrival out of the lane of men, women and children, who have knelt on either side for his blessing. It is all very simple; like our sister water, *e multo utile et humile et pretiosa et casta.*

It was barely half-past eleven when Allison slipped in through the choir-door, but the church was already densely peopled. Monseigneur had come in before him and was before the high alter beginning the mass *Dominus Dixit.* Allison wandered vainly down one aisle and up the other, and at last found a foothold on the altar steps of a Chapel, far up on the Epistle side. By craning his neck he could, through a glass screen, see some part of the sanctuary; but he must manoeuvre his feet clear of a party of babies drowsing on the Chapel floor. A dog, introduced there for some reason of convenience, lurked aware in the corner. Since the war began Allison had never seen so many people in any one place; but never had he felt so cleanly alone. One by one torturing memories, regret, shame, doubt, desire, slipped off him; war or peace, life or death, there was nothing else but this. Then quickly, but without abruptness, he became part of that vast pondering crowd, which began to surge forward like the sea-swell in a harbour, to the choir rails: there he saw the old shepherd feed his flock. Half-an-hour passed, or an hour; still they came quietly to the pasture. A woman whispered *Monseigneur se sauve. Il est trop fatigué.* Allison looked, the Bishop had gone back to his seat by the altar, the snowy heads of his Canons were still bent over the rails, and their voices murmured continuously.

III.

The midnight Communion was ended. Monseigneur, returned to the altar, had begun the mass *Lux Fulgebit.* Two o'clock had struck, and the crowd began to surge out into the darkened town. With a little group between the Choir and Sacristy, Allison waited. At last all was over; the silken umbrella, yellow as its old ivory handle, was brought from its corner and raised in expectation. The little old Bishop appeared underneath it. In a few hours he would have returned to the altar to sing the Pontifical High Mass of Christmas Day. Meanwhile, we must all seek our beds. The little knot of worshippers fell to their knees and pressed forward into a line on each side of him. This way and that, from one man's lips to another's went the jewelled hand; the fingers blessed us, the kind eyes smiled.

Allison made his way up to the embankment, crossed the cold, chattering Paillon by one of its bridges and began to climb the long hill to Cimiez. He may have been the worst man in France that day, but he was among the happiest.

IV.

Next afternoon between the dashes of rain, Allison and the Musical Genius, composer and accompanist of our party, made their way down the Roman path from Cimiez to the River, and so up to the old Castellum. Standing by its summit, they looked down on the City and saw Nice with new eyes. In the foreground a clash of bells and drifting chimney smoke; and then, piled in utter confusion, green, black, brown, red, yellow and all washed bright by the morning's rain, were the roofs of the Old Town. There seemed no room for any streets, even the well-known "Places," the flower market, that one by the Cathedral and others through which they had just climbed were hidden beyond discovery. The Paillon (broad enough under its bridges) showed a thin line, like the parting in a man's hair, between them and the sharper edges of the New Town beyond. Far off, where the river dived into its tunnels beneath the Casino, a bustle of trams showed, small and fussy, in the Place Massena. This was a Nice we had not known nor conjectured . . . But it grew dark and chilly. Even here winter had found us out. In a few days, cured of convalescence, we should be adorning the messes of our several Base Depots. In a few more we should be telling tales about it all, each in his regiment. Meanwhile, we must be getting back to Cimiez, to change and dine before our performance.

BRAMANTIP.

Published in The New Witness, December 14, 1916

IV. DARKENED YPRES AND THE WAY OUT

This paper is an immediate sequel to that called "Hallowe'en" the last part of which appeared on November 9, 1916. The events here described happened in November, 1914. Their author having returned to France, has not corrected the proofs of this article, nor can he promise regularity in the appearance of its successors.

The shortest way to Ypres was by the Kemmell road on through Vierstraat and Kruisstraathock; but that road being apparently out of order we paraded, early on November 6, on the Poperinghe Road and marched as far as the cross-road south of Locre, where our own Brigade, appearing from Bailleul, was presently to absorb us. We had come out of our last adventure quite easily and marched north with some confidence to carry on the campaign so magnificently (as we had already heard) begun in Belgium by the Seventh Division. We sat an hour or more there; some of our packs in the ditch – there was snow in it. One in a hundred yards, more fortunate, found seat-hold on a hectometre stone. At last the Brigade came in sight, across a dip in the ground to our left, and they moved up the road that converged, a little ahead of us, with their own. As they passed the cross-roads we fell in and followed them; our destination remained uncertain, but we knew well that there had been fighting, all last month, round Ypres. Allison was detailed, by his new company commander – who had arrived from England during our four days in billets – to take a small party of D Company in rear of the Brigade, and to pick up and urge forward stragglers. Unfortunately the men allotted him proved to be born stragglers every one; and, as afternoon wore on, a whole Army Corps seemed to have crept on to the road between him and his regiment.

Several field ambulances and at least three mounted chaplains had passed him when at last he got his party wedged in front of a large wagon, with orders not to fall behind it. The paved roadway was just wide enough for the waggon – on each side of it an uninviting morass *reserve aux piétons*. These were afterwards timbered and allowed a firm passage, but in this mild week of November, 1914, between a frost and a frost there was nothing but the unfathomable mud of Belgium, until, north of Dickebusch, the vicinal railway reappeared and formed a kind of footpath into the town. Allison's party, soon divided by the waggon, ploughed on through the mud for some way on each side and reformed on the *pave* behind it. In despair he called a five minute's halt, and gave them a piece of his mind; but without much success.

"I beg yer pardon, sir," answered an old Jock firmly, "a man cannot keep pace with a horse."

Coming at last, at dusk, to the side of Dikebusch Pond, Allison discovered that the Duke of Rothesay's had taken a lane to the left and were resting; as he joined them an order came round that the Battalion would not move until half-past six. Two men per platoon might fetch water – source unknown – for tea. Tea sounded pleasant. We had done long march in hours if not in miles that day, and were not yet much more than half-way to our new position; we were sitting roughly in line, along the edges of two or three fields, while a woolly white mist rolled over us. Far away, to the north, beyond Elverdinghe, sounded the occasional "humph" of a heavy gun.

II.

Almost before the water-carriers had disappeared in the mist new orders reached us. The Battalion would move on at once. Allison was detailed again to stay behind; this time to collect the odd men as they came in and bring them along in rear of the Battalion. They returned by degrees, were collected and marched off by Allison; and after dodging past various columns of transport, found the

Duke of Rothesay's halted where three ways meet at this end of Kruisstraat, and so were able to rejoin their companies.

It was very dark now, and cold. On all sides of us rifle-fire could be heard; nearer came a strange clatter; and a chance light from the village showed the plumed and burnished helmets a squadron of French cavalry. At last we were in a town and marching along streets full of rubbish. Wheeling right, the whole column was suddenly involved in a maze of fallen telegraph wires. Clear of these, we were in a long street of shuttered houses. Here and there candle-light showed through the grating of a cellar – but in the streets we met no one. At last we were in a great open space. The headlights of a passing General's car showed, on our left the long arcaded front of a great civic building. Its main tower was still shrouded in scaffolding; its statues looked down, unscathed still, from their niches. Just behind us, on the left, a wire fence enclosed a deep shell hole in the pavement. "What a race of swine!" Allison exclaimed, as he saw it. "Cathedrals I can understand their shelling, but a building like this, purely commercial, the finest in the world of its kind, but the one sort of thing they might themselves do well . . . I suppose it's jealousy—" At this point, to the Captain's unconcealed delight, the speaker disappeared into another and deeper shell hole, which, lurking on their right flank, he had not observed as he marched, rhapsodising, past the Cloth Hall of Ypres.

BRAMANTIP
Published in The New Witness, January 4th, 1917

III.

At the Menin gate we crossed a bridge and were on a straight road, edged with tall trees, which, we imagined, ran straight forward into the enemy's lines. Where the town ended, we fell out again and rested for two hours; the road was covered here with a snowy slush, but some of us managed, balancing their heads and heels on the lines of the Vicinal railway, and covering the gap with a ground sheet, to make a bed it was just worth our while to lie down on. In time the word came that we might get straw from a stack about two fields to our left; and a melancholy procession was felt rather than seen to be straggling through deep mud in an uncertain line, until the stack was found, and then returning with stiff armfuls of congealed straw.

Leaving the Menin road where the railway crosses it, at a Halte whose name has clean escaped me, we marched on through the ruins of Zillebeke into a dense wood, and about six in the morning came to a line of little holes in each of which a weary soldier awaited our relieving him. It was nearly twenty four hours since we had left our billet at Deschildre's. Allison was almost too sleepy to think which of the sleepy men under his command should first go on sentry. Another problem arose. Water was only to be had at a pump in a farmyard some way off; and should not be fetched during daylight. As always, in the weariest moments, instant decisions had to be made; then we all sank into our little holes, dug, it seemed, by individual enterprise with the entrenching tool; and ressembling a set of moulds in which bath chairs might be cast.

Here we sat for a fortnight while the world got news of the first Battle of Ypres. At first we had no communication with each other unless by walking overland through a clearing in the wood. In time we connected our holes into a formless sort of trench, without parados of traverses; we even dug a few short boyaux through the clearing into the shelter of the trees behind. While the dry weather lasted, we were happy enough. But one night Allison – sleeping for half an hour on a scatter of pinetops in a dead end of his trench, his head poked into a hollow six inches deep, which was all we had then to call "dug-outs" – awoke, dreaming that the world was ended, to find that his head cover, loosened by heavy rain, had fallen into his open mouth. In that hour winter overtook us. A little road crossing our line at right angles gave the next trouble. As the rain fell, it filtered through the soil and so ran beneath the floor of our trench where it cut through the road. Suddenly like the crust of a pie the trench rose to the road's level, seeming still to offer a good footing; but woe to the soldier who stepped there. After that the snow came plentifully upon us.

IV.

I have said little, yet, of the enemy. He lay very near but rather below us. As the ground behind us was flat he could not, from in front, see us walking there, while we had cover from the wood on each side. As our line was drawn back a little from the edge of the flat ground we could no more see him, unless we went out to find him, a procedure in which Bob soon grew expert. We had just been given our first bombs – empty jam-tins refilled and fuzed – with private instructions to bury them in some quiet place if they were not successful. The enemy, on the other hand, had brought trench mortars, whose projectiles lurched visibly through the air above us, fell and lay buried some seconds before exploding. Their effect was not pleasant. Men were apt to be buried rather too long in the half-frozen mud before they could be dug out of it; those who were came out with shattered nerves, sometimes speechless. We developed a plan of crooking our elbows in front of our faces when the mortars came, so that if we were buried we might keep a breathing space. What we liked least was the idea that our skulls might be "opened in error" by a rescuer's pick.

The young officer of 1917, brought up on the catechism "Is your wire strong enough?" will be amused by our defences in that time. A single line of barbed wire running from tree to tree and looped round them; cut almost nightly by rifle fire and repaired next morning "between the sun and the sky," that was all. But we had a stronger defence. Our shells and the enemy's crossing frequently overhead brought down many trees of the wood about our ears.

In front of "D" Company's line this barricade was impenetrable. During our fortnight in the first Battle of Ypres I do not think that a single German entered the Duke of Rothesay's lines, nor a Jock of ours into theirs.

V.

In the small hours of the twentieth, we were relieved. Reduced in strength as we were, two battalions combined to relieve us. One of these consisted of one officer and about a hundred men. We were too anxious to get out, to see a fire and to taste warmed food, to have much sympathy – or interest even in less fortunate regiments. After a heartrending march along forest rides knee-deep in a very viscous mud, we closed up in fours on the Menin road, still facing towards Menin. A short march brought us in sight (there must have been a moon) of houses – a spectral row they stood, perhaps twenty feet high, but not more than eight feet deep, theirs roofs rising from the road to their back wall which descended abruptly from top to bottom. The row was broken by a great pair of gates, wrought in iron with coronets and cyphers; and Allison guessed that the houses belonged to the squire and principally furnished shelter for his fruit trees. Here – although the village was Hooge – we felt safe and comfortable. Fires were lighted, rations given out; tired but happy, and quite aware that we had (most unreasonably) held up for ever the advance on Calais, we slept till dawn.

BRAMANTIP
Published in The New Witness: January 11th , 1917

ON BEING WOUNDED

It is extremely interesting to have seen the business of being wounded from the point of view of a casualty. For those who only know the wounded soldier as a carefully washed individual ministered to by efficient nurses and seen against the staged background of a ward filled with sunlight and bright flowers, the reality of the thing cannot exist. The visitor is deceived by the "astonishing cheerfulness" of the patient – perhaps his sole exhibition of animation during the day – and, out of a justifiable feeling that this cannot be all, sets against this picture the most improbable and erroneous imaginations as to the frightfulness of what is under the bandages.

But it is doubtful whether the man himself can make any more accurate an estimation of his condition. There is a continuous, insensible shifting of the perspective from the moment that he feels the thud made by the arrival of the bullet to that when he realises one day at the end of his convalescence, that he is well again. The gradual changes are so subtle, the inability to reproduce any one state of consciousness when in the next is so complete that the most introspective must hope for nothing better than confused reminiscence. One feels the analogy with the point of focus of a microscope, which passes through successive layers of an object, each layer being the only one existing for one at the time. So that if this slight record be somewhat incoherent it may at least serve to reflect something of the confusion of feelings which called it forth.

Apart from the actual physical injury, the most interesting fact about being hit, and probably the one which makes the experience as difficult to digest, is the abrupt transition from a life of incessant strain and action to one of complete inactivity. The engine is abruptly stopped – dead. How can one hope to accommodate oneself to such a change? So there is in the minds of the people in the field dressing-station the most exhausting swinging between speculations as to what is going to happen to them individually, and what is to be the fate of the battalion, battery or squadron they have just left. I have seen artillery officers nearly weeping at the thought that while they lay impotent their battery was at last, after months of waiting, moving forward in pursuit. Did the mine go off? Did we take the wood? Did all our other aeroplanes get back? These are the absorbing considerations, from which willy-nilly one is paradoxically brought back to the contemplation of a battered foot or a shrapnel spattered arm. (This applies to all but those seriously hit; for them there is often merciful unconsciousness.)

As the hours go by more and more strands become entwined in the pattern. Very soon there appears, as a sudden realisation, the thought that "this" mean "Blighty" – perhaps for months. And one whispers "London" almost reverently. It is a splendid moment. Perhaps one has found oneself by this time in an ambulance – the whole experience is so steeped in unreality, anyway, that one accepts the change unwonderingly – and there begin conjectures about Hospital. But we may not think too long: there come attempts at sleep, or periods during which impressions are taken in a quite unquestioning, passive way. There is a pleasure in the lazy exercise of the senses, so that the wounded man may find himself continuously stroking the edge of his blanket or regarding without comment or conjecture yet with deep, inexplicable satisfaction, the people and places he is passing on the road.

By the time the clearing-hospital is reached, by continual bumping and jolting about, there is an intense desire for rest, for that spotlessly white bed which has bulked so largely in his active-service dreams. Peace, however, is not yet; the wound is dressed and *via* more stretchers one is pushed onto an ambulance train for the base hospital. Another strand is interwoven; the insignificance of one wounded man when in the grip of a system which handles the unending stream of casualties with the indifference of a universal store. There are walking cases and stretcher cases, and on each man is pinned a large luggage label designating him concisely and accurately. As such he is pushed on and off stretchers, dumped in odd corners of draughty railway stations, stacked in rows on ambulance trains, but all the time nearing an increasingly vivid England. These journeys sometimes last nearly twenty-four hours: there accordingly follow interminable conversations which arise easily enough when each member of the party carries on his person the wherewithal to cause interesting discussion. The formula is unvarying:

"Where did you get it?"

"Left leg."

Here the questioner usually says "No, I mean what part of the line?" – "Oh! Monchy," and the rest is easy. Never before came so strongly the feeling that this eager mutual handing over of small change is not indulged for the sake of the little facts that one learns in the process; it is a reaching out, an adult substitute for the action of children who walk securely hand-in-hand. To the sick man it is the greatest sedative he has.

All this time the pain has, so to speak, been given out in a subdued manner by the double bass, but when the white bed is finally attained and the excitements of the journey are fading, with all the rapidity with which, for the patient, all impressions seem to fade, it begins to be announced with more insistence.

Then begins that alternation of exaltation and depression which is so bewildering to recall afterwards. There is a timeless element in it; so that when in pain there seems to exist for one only the pain already suffered and that inevitably to come. And when the leg has ceased to throb or the daily dressing is happily over, the mind wanders over all the pleasant things of the peace and anticipates the future peace of impending convalescence. In each state the other appears inconceivable – it is as if one were changed suddenly from a black bishop, moving freely about the black squares of the chess-board, into a white one, for whom blackness does not exist.

Wounds, however, quickly grow less painful and the ordinary

case is in a week or so ready to be transferred to England. Again there is the mixing on ambulance trains and boat with men of all regiments and with as many different kinds of wounds. Curiosity about one another is unabated; again I have to explain either that I was wounded in the leg or at Arras – according to the demands of my questioner. At last – submarines permitting – one reaches Victoria. This should be tremendous, but by this time one is too limp to do more than purr appreciatively. But the spectacle of taxicabs, parks, delightful old gentlemen who raise their hats at the sight of the ambulance, is quite unforgettable. Arras seems inconceivably remote. Then the stretcher for the last time and one is in an English bed.

Thus I arrived on the first spring day of 1917, and was turning on my side thankfully to sleep, when from the opposite bed came the question:

"*Where did you get it?!!*"

With a feeling of sinister foreboding I made a desperate choice. "At Arras."

"No! no!" he said, "I mean . . .!"

It was probably inevitable.

L.H

Published in the New Witness, July 12th , 1917

EARLY POEMS
1905–1909

God – And One Man – Make a Majority

'Twas here the antient Church in days forgotten
    Built her an house wherein to praise thee: now
The trees that rose upon its site are rotten
    In turn-unchanged alone remainest-Thou

I will fight for Thee if I may fight with Thee:
    Against our strength what mortal might endure?
Make me thine armour-bearer, Lord, but prithee
    Let none reproach me that I am not pure.

What God have cleansed may no man call common
    Then cleanse me Lord that I be clean and fair;
So may Thy Son who scorned not Birth of Woman
    Enter my Heart and make His Temple there.

To David Clutterbuck

Agnes Dead in Martholm

"Cousin, the sun that was so bright
        Is set now; weary day
Flies forth before this darkling night.
        Seen clear where fields are grey,
O'er Martholm brook curled mist hang white;
        So come, let us away!

"Further, of Martholm wood have I
        Heard many a tale of old;
How strange shapes fly 'neath God's blind sky
        When winter nights are cold,
How all that sees them surely die.
        Maids may not be so bold---"

"I have vowed a vow by Holy Rood
        And by God's Mother dear,
To move nor stir from Martholm wood
        Ere to-morrow's sun appear.
No fiend hath no power to harm the good
        Who praying banish fear."

Thus answered Agnes Ladyelys
        To her cousin, Joan oth' Fen,
And ceased; there came a little breeze
        And stirred the tree-tops then;
Beneath the murmur of the trees
        Joan answered her again: —

"Ever, within my Father's hall,
    Is there not room for thee?
Yea, though his lands be poor and small,
    He hath none to his care but me;
He has floor and roof more firm withal
    Than these dank woods may be."

"Cousin, I prithee ask me not
    Lest my too weak heart turn,
For I have won to this dark spot
    Firmly intent to learn
What shall be my lot and his lot
    For that my heart doth burn.

Tonight it is All Hallows Even
    When the dear ghost of the dead
From scarlet Hell, from golden Heaven,
    Troop earthward, and 'tis said
To him who sees them here is given
    His future life to read.

And lo! This sooth came to my ear
    When winter chilled the ground;
I hoped throughout the unwinding year
    And, ever hoping, found
No cure for care, save coming here,
    To watch by the ghastly mound.

(A mighty king, a Northern king
    Was slain in clashing fight.
Hither to burial did they bring
    His body from men's sight.
Yet men have seen him, still walking
    Weary throughout the night.

I too may see him.) . . . But depart!
    Long since thou shouldst be gone.
Thy Father knows not where thou art;
    Go: for he loves thee, Joan . . ."
Came little fears, gnawing her heart,
    And passed. She was alone.

No simple words of prayer she said
    Kneeling, and when she could
No longer pray, then raised her head;
    And all aghast she stood.
For lo! The pale feet of the dead
    Walked past her through the wood.

The moon, by glittering bars of rain
    Each way prolonged, scarce shone
Now, along some long cloud- let lane
    Looked with chilled eyes and wan;
Now, drawing dreamily down again
    Through close cloud- gates was gone.

Sudden she saw her father's ghost
    Whom banded men had ta'en
In war against a robber host;
    Yet slaying was he slain.
Now through his eyes his soul burned, lost
    In a world of deathless pain.

She ran to meet him, but, at thought
    Of him, she durst not ask.
He might not know the thing she sought,
    Might scorn her heart-set task;
And in her brain his eyes blazed, wrought
    Of flame through a still mask.

Her mother next moved into sight;
      (Ah! Sweet, sad memories!)
From all her head there gleamed a light
      Known only to the eyes
Of those that have passed to God's bright
      City in Paradise.

"Mother, from where thou see'st all,
      From God's right hand above,
Hast seen what fortune shall befall
      Thy daughter, and what love?"
Silent, the mother sighed, and all
      Tall trees sighed round the grove.

She vanished; and a third came by.
      "Madonna, who is this?
I know the form, the face, the eye
      I know, for they are his!"
She saw her fate. Were she to die
      They'd meet where no death is.

Silent she rose and left the mound;
      (Never a word she said.)
A place of leaves for a couch she found,
      And prayed, bowing her head . . ..
When the rain-dimmed hour of the sun drew round
      Joan seeking found her, dead.

Written March 1906
Verse added November 1907
Published in New Field No.3.
Nov. 1907

Hylas.

Heracles absent, Hylas left his oar
Sent to despoil the Naiads' antient home;
But they delayed him; till Aegean foam
Was cloven again and again round Argo. More and more
Marvelling, Heracles in turn must roam
And cry, till, mocking him, the breaker's war
Seemed turned to Hylas, till the bent grey shore
The pine green mountains echoed "Hylas! Come!"

Yet he came not. Lies he on some green bed
Mute trophy of their fruitless victory
That round him mourn? Perhaps he is not dead
But rules their region, and is fancied free
While lank-stemmed lilies, wreathed about his head,
Rise to the air and plead for liberty.

Written 1906
Wykhamist. No. 439. Nov 1906
Academy 10. Viii. 07
To Robert Ross

Untitled

Mark now his body stiffening to the leap
   The cry, the fiery line of flashing limb
The water rising to the kiss of him
The lingering green bubbles, which his deep
Kingdom that lurks untrodden 'neath the pool
   Has sent to bit their tyrant tarry there,
   To light his path- to tell him he is fair
(So could not we have told him?)
                White and cool

Now he emerges. All the joyful grass,
     Trembling and breaking in flowers at his feet,
     With wondrous fragrance notes where he shall pass;
While we, his fellow-men, worship, alas
   In silence, whom we dare not run to greet.
   Yea – but to worship him alone – how sweet!

Untitled

I was the Prince's page: and he
Was more than all the world to me.

Down the street the young Prince rode
Very fair for the eye to see
My head was bowed to my heart's grave load
No woman turned her to smile at me
I was but the Prince's page: and he
the cause of all my misery.

As he gaily rode through the fond, hot night
To squander his gold and the kingly blood
could he not know that his heart's delight
Was to me as a worm in a virgin bud?
I was but the Prince's page: not good
Nor great enough to be understood.

So soon we came to the cursèd gate
Wherethrough he would pass to heart's desire
(She was not as good even as I – not as great
But she sucked his soul with lips of fire.
I was but the Prince's page: with a hire
Given freely to turn me to fool and liar.

"But why hast thou spurned the love that I gave

    (O my master, my heart's chrised? King!)

I reasoned- and shortly, again grown brave,

      Clasped his knees, crying "Master, do not this thing –"

           Then paused, and looked up in his eyes,
              drawing breath.

           (I looked for love and he gave me death!)

    What had I, the Prince's page, done to bring

    His wrath on me thus? .... Ere my soul takes wing

For a kinglier court let him know that then, even then I forgave.

To James Stewart Wilson

Epilogue

No linkèd hum of passing-bell
No sound of turnèd beads may tell
His death that knew them over well.

Dying the comfortable word
He'd loved through life he never heard:

No secret rites of oil or Mass-
Unaided, God helped him to pass.

Not in the sun's nor taper's light
But through the quiet of the night

Ere e'en the matins of the lark
His soul strode forth into the dark.

Untitled

Cold is Earth and sky and sea;
     Every bough on every tree
Cold 'neath snow hangs heavily:
     Yet 'tis joyous Christmas morn
And now to sing of Jesus
And Mary- Queen will please us,
Maid Mary, Jesu's Mother,
     Of whom our Christ was born.

  O let us sing a cheerful strain,
     Our Lord to-day is born again.

Though no bird sings today,
Though snow beguiles our way,
  Though cheerless now all earth is:
Sing we laud to Mary Mother,
Than whom to ne'er another
  More joy of Jesu's birth is.
     Now, in this bitter season,
     Sing *"Maria Eleeson."*

In a stable was He born
To her on blessed Christmas morn
  By a city of the East, that Bethlam hight;
And dull shepherds came in wonder
And did bend the rough knee under
  Whom an angel guided thither, through the night.
     Singing *"Christie Eleeson"*
     As they had good reason.

Swarth kings of Eastern races,
Great joy in hearts on faces,
Had left their rich palaces
    Taught by a star to welcome Him to Earth;
Which as saw, the Child
Of Mary undefiled
Uprasied his hand and smiled,
    Blessing as now, His servants at His Birth.
        Wherefore our song that swells is
        "Gloria in Excelsis"

Written: July 1907 – Published: "Pageant Post" Oxford; July – 1907

Love's Kalendar

Where your tall pine stood thatched in snows
    We heard soft feathers move:
Our eyes in startled concert rose.
    Lo! From the boughs above
        Laughed little Love.

I made for him a mansion warm
    Safe in your sheltering breast;
Till Spring he would devise no harm,
    But slumber silent, lest
        He lost that rest.

In May he summoned secretly
    My eyes to gaze in yours,
While, innocent of anguish, we
    Lived amid censing flowers
        Days that seemed hours.

But, when increasing suns of June
    Laid heat behind the sky,
And nightly mocked the needless moon,
    Love chose to droop and die
        Nor know July.

So now I, left alone, alas!
　　In dreams see your one frown,
While on the rare, sun-strangled grass
　　Leaves, weather-worn and brown,
　　　　Lie lightly down.

A.L.H

Written July 1907
Published New Field No.2. October 1907
P 21
To the Honourable George Dawson-Damer

Sunset in West Flanders

The drowsy sun that shuts his house
     Draws dusk across these dunes
      Whence float on silence weird, unworded tunes
          Of childish ritual . . .
Behind their drooping sunflower-wall
Grumble great sows.

Harshly a Flemish Mother speaks
     Two Flemish infants wail;
      While, heaving high each warped and rusted sail
      To hurl it down amain,
          The mill, convulsed with antient pain,
Shudders and shrieks.

Then- as amid the streets' hoarse hum
     A cart-dogs' vehement note
      Has with deep red thunder filled his long red throat
      -Before he goes to bed
      The sun parts curtains, shows his head
And all are dumb.

Written: November 1907
Published: New Field no 5
March 1908 pp6–7
To Miss (Mary Katherine) Daphne

THE BURDEN OF
Bartimew: the which
Was blind, and
Seeth.

Timew his blind-son am I,
That dwell in Hiericho city;
And blind was I right from my birth,
Abas'd of all men here on earth,
Till one day the dear Lord did go,
And those twelve friends, through Hiericho.
And as I sate beside that gate,
Where day by day I ever sate,
I heard a mighty sound of men,
Passing me by the whole day then;
And thus I heard, a wight did say: ---
    "The blessed Iesus, comes this way!"
Then all the people 'gan shout "Hail
To Xt the King of Israel!
Hosanna!" Of a sudden, I
Uttered a mighty piteous cry,
    "Lord, Heal my eyn or that I die!"
They trode me under foot: they hushed
My voice; they pressed me and they pushed
And smote me, saying most sternly,
    "Much thou deservest, man to die;
Why troublest thou the Master? Go
Thy way at once from Hiericho!"
But He who rules the angels (there
In Heaven) heard my humble prayer.
Nor heeded He their clownish taunt,
But bade me ask him all my want.
    "Sweet Lord," I said, "To gain my sight,
To live so, as men live, in light,

Is my desire." The Lord straightly
Lifted the cloud from either eye;
So allthing now I see clearly,
And ever, till that day I die,
Will praise the Lord exceedingly,
SIRE, SON and GHOST, Blest Trinity.

A.L.H.

A Mother's Prayer

Beautiful James Alison,
        What thing have you done?
I am your Mother and
        You my one son.
Is it naught to you that
        My days in fasting pass,
My nights in prayer and weeping
        For you, my son. Alas
You never loved your mother
        As she you, James;
But kindled in another
        Unhallowed flames.-
-Who can tell for certain
        The death that he shall die
Drawing fate's close curtain?
        Neither you nor I!
But you have kindled flames
        And in flames your ghost shall burn,
And all your vaunted beauty, James,
        To leprous ashes turn.
Then James Alison
        Will have played his part
And this thing over all have done-
        Broken his mother's heart.

Published: New Field
No 7. April; 1908.

To Lord Fredrick Conyngham

Lines written in the Kardomah

A Child- athirst to stand admired:
A Boy- aflame to feel desired:
A Man- ashamed of Youth's delight;-
Awake to wish the world good-night-
Asleep to dream of sin and sorrow,
And how the Book will read tomorrow.

Written: June 12th 1909

Telephones antient and modern

When by the coolness of thy shrine
Father, I knelt and called thy name
My soul burned with the sincere flame
Of a glad lamp that sees clear wine
Flow into Love's mysterious blood.
But my heart burned some worldlier way.
Shame dared not love, sin would not pray.—
My feet, where late his feet had stood,
Ached . . . . . . All that morning (had I known!)
His voice along the telephone
Had hummed in search of me. And so
We spoke. By nightfall it was well-
Men praise new science. But I know
Thy antient ways as laudable.

Written: Edinburgh: Macvitties: July 1909
To the dead Bishop W.W.

To a Public Man

I have admired so your life
So watcht you on your curious way!
I am too male to be your wife
And most I look towards the day
When, slightly leaner in the loin,
Strippt of your pretty pants and paints,
Death shall dispatch you, dear, to join
A cunning company of saints.
Then will my prayers like smoke descend
And melt like well developed dew.
Ask Satan, please, to be my friend:-
He would do anything for you—

Oxford 17. Viii. 1909

On a Roman Road

(For a set of verses written for the music of C.A.G)

I
Far before us through the night
Gleams the highway straight and white;
Splits for us the lowering down;
Echoes our steps in the town.

Pilgrim centuries have passed
Down its vistas and at last
Vanished over the hill-brow,
Whither years are hurrying now.

Minutes chased by minutes hide
Rustling along the green roadside.
Whether we advance or stay
Night will leave us soon today.

Cottages will open their eyes;
Birds will twitter; smoke will rise.
Our way lies across the down
To the crumbling, crimson town.

Untitled

Go lightly over him, vain carpeters
    That of this green place, holds a little length
Forget, regarding, as you read my verse
    How great their theme, how puny these words strength

But oh! Disturb him not; his quiet soul
    Knows not, frequently, here, another harbor
Strange forest gods, instant in whose control
The meek ground bears your crude and gaudy arbours.

Build you up high; but let me stand beneath
    I'll see the pomp here and the majesty
"God save King George" I'll say with quiet breath
    "Queen Mary save him"- when the people cry-

And praying still I will not heed their cheers
For my King, George, still passes lingering here.

WAR POEMS

Billeted

We're in billets again, and tonight, if you please,
I shall strap myself up in a Wolseley valise;
What's that, boy? Your boots give you infinite pain?
You can chuck them away, we're in billets again.

We're in billets again now, and, barring alarms,
There'll be no occasion for standing to arms;
And I've often observed, with night-watches to keep,
That the hour before daylight's the best hour for sleep.

We're feasting on chocolate, game pie, currant bun,
To a faint German-band obligato of gun,
For I've noticed, wherever the regiment go,
That we always end up pretty close to the foe.

But we're clean out of reach of trench mortars and snipers
Five inches south-west of the "esses" in Ypres.
(Old Bob who knows better, pronounces it Yper,
Don't argue the point now, you'll waken the sleeper.)

The patron brings beer up, our thirst for to quench
So we'll drink him good fortune in English and French;
Bob, who finds my Parisian accent a blemish,
Goes one better himself in a torrent of Flemish.

It's a fortnight on Sunday since Antony died
And John's at Boulogne with a hole in his side;
While poor Harry's got lost, the Lord only knows where –
May the Lord keep them all and ourselves in His care.

Mustn't think we don't mind when a chap gets laid out,
They've taken the best of us, never a doubt;
But with life pretty busy, and death rather near
We've no time for regret any more than for fear.

Here's luck to our host, Isidore Deschildre,
Himself and his wife and their numerous childer;
And the brave contrebandier that bays our return;
More power to his paws when he treads by the churn.

You may go to the Ritz or the Curzon (Mayfair)
And think they do things pretty well for you there;
When you've lain for six weeks on a water-logged plain
Here's the acme of luxury – billets again."

Neuve Eglise November 1914

Domum

The green and gray and purple day is battered with clouds of
    dun
From ruined Ypres smouldering beneath the sun,
Another hour will see it flower (lamentable sight)
A bush of burning roses underneath the night.
Who will fight for Flanders, who will set them free,
The war-worn lowlands by the English sea?
Who my young companions, will choose the way to war
That Marlborough, Wellington, have trodden out before?

Are those mere names? Then hear a solemn sound,
The blood of our brothers is crying from the ground:
"What we dared and suffered, what the rest may do,
Little sons of Wykeham, is it nought to you?"

"Father and Founder, our feet may never more
Tread the stones of Flint Court or Gunner's green shore;
But whatever they assemble we are pressing near,
Calling and calling-could our brothers hear!"

Brothers they have heard you, see them leaving their
School, Meads, River, for camp and barrack square;
And all the gold their futures hold in youth's abundant store
They'd freely give to have you live in their midst once more.

What was it that you fought for; Why was it that you died?
Here is Ypres burning, and twenty towns beside.
Where is the gain in all our pain when we have loved but now
Is lying still on Sixty Hill, a bullet in his brow?

He died one thing believing, that is better worth
Than the golden cities of all the kings on earth,
Were right and wrong to choose among he knew to choose the
    right
He found the task appointed, and did it with his might.
So I muse regarding, with a pensive eye
Towered Ypres blazing beneath the midnight sky.
That way may lie failure: but towers there are that stand –
Here, it may be, guarded, in our own green land.

Domum was written in 1915 and published in an anthology of War Poetry collected by A E Osborn in 1917 called "The Muse in Arms."

The Field of Honour

Mud-Stained and rain-sodden, a sport for flies and lice,
Out of this vilest life into vile death he goes;
His grave will soon be ready, where the grey rat knows
There is fresh meat slain for her;- our mortal bodies rise,
In those foul scampering bellies, quick – and yet, those eyes
That stare on life still out of death, and will not close,
Seeing in a flash the Crown of Honour, and the Rose
Of Glory wreathed about the Cross of Sacrifice,
Died radiant. May some English traveller to-day
Leaving his city cares behind him, journeying West
To the brief solace of a sporting holiday
Quicken again with boyish ardour, as he sees,
For a moment, Windsor castle towering on the crest
And Eton still enshrined among remembered trees.

Written: 1916
Published in 1917 in 'The Muse in Arms'

Only Child

When I have said my prayers
Nurse always goes downstairs,
She laughs to see her supper, and I don't suppose she cares
Whether I'm asleep or waking,
Though the noise the maids are making
Sets the windows rattling and the door, and the four walls shaking.

Then in the room before me stands
The boy that has the warmest hands
And the coldest heart of any in the bright night lands:
It's he that makes bad faces
In the dark, damp places
Till I get no sleep with frightening at those bold grimaces.

So deft he is and cunning,
Very soon he gets me running
Over fields and woods and rivers, but of course we're only funning.
Then we fly, so fleet and airy,
Til we meet the Queen of Faery:
And her face is like the photographs of poor Aunt Mary.

She asks, have I been good
And done all the things I should;
So I say I've learned my lessons, and had tea, p'haps in the wood.
But that cruel boy I am facing
On the word begins grimacing;
And she vanishes; and soon the path we start retracing.

When a thousand miles we've sped
I am back beside my bed,
And my little body lying there, as quiet as the dead;
Then I creep inside, and wait
Til nurse rattles at the grate,
And I know she's had her supper, and the hour is growing late.
So I lie til darkness ends;

But my night is full of friends
Who shew me things and take me off sometimes – but that depends.
Then my coloured sky turns white,
And the nursery's full of light,
And the kettle boiling, and the birds on the wall, all bright.

Written in May 1917 in France, severely wounded and with shell shock.
The little boy is Death, from whom he has just managed to escape.
Published in The New Witness, January 24th 1918

Aftersong

The queerest thing of all now, is the way the sizes shift, Johnny;
    Bracken Hill's no height now, no height at all.
And the little dog Peter was the weight I just could lift,
      He's grown to hide mountains, but the great dog's starved
      and small.

Deep enough's the pool to swim now where for rocks we
    wouldn't dive, Johnny;
    But the river that we'd never leap, it's no step over now,
And the wild bull's field we used to pass, the time I was alive,
    I can lean across the hedge of it and scratch its brow.

Step-mother's so little and queer, I needn't ever cry, Johnny,
    And her cruel way of talking leaves me easy in my rest:
But you I can't see all at once, you're grown so high;
      And that's because the heart's great that struggles in your
      breast.

Written 1917 with the title 'The Return'
Published as 'Aftersong' in the New Witness, September 20, 1918

The Face of Raphael

With so much to do that day we found no time to pause and pray;
For none contrived an hour to borrow from endless leisure earned
    the morrow.
But as the quick Spring sun faded, lightening homewards we
    paraded
Quietly in our barrack-square, and marched to battle, unaware
What was keeping step with us..Coelistis exercitus;
Who watched with us upon the hill called Monchy, slumbering
    not, until
Night's last blue was broken with a crimson sentence, spoken
By a thousand guns in chorus; and dawn and battle lay before us;
Till with dayspring shells crashed above us – let them now pray
    well that love us.
Following them the lurid sky, gently hastening went they, I,
Like a pailful of water thrown from a high window, fell . . . Alone.

An hour or two I lay and dozed, my unattempting features closed,
Or opened a reluctant eye to search the irresponsive sky,
Not speaking, while my dull ears heard many a just-remembered
    word
Twine themselves into a song, tuneless'
Here beginneth
That old lesson, earth to earth turns, and death regards birth,
Nothing of us but doth fade utterly . . .

. . . Ah, whose mind prayed
Through mine then? Whose quiet singing heard I from my
   stretcher, swinging
Sorry, weary, sick, belated back to Arras? Who dictated
Strongly, clearly, till I sung these French words with my English
   tongue?
"In the dim hour of life and death, when the slow agony is begun,
And the soul scans with faltering breath that hard road whereby heaven
   is won:

Oh, that we might with Tobit, when, seeking the child of Raguel,
Prudent and coy, the homes of men he left; in one clear instant see
-With a proud smile to call us hence where the darkness gathers dense
Of each his Mesopotamy; constant, compassionate, intense,
The face of Raphael!"

Written 1917 when he was wounded at Monchy le Preux

Silver Badgeman

Houses I hate now, who have seen houses strewn,
A bitter matter for battle, by sun and by moon:
Stones crumbled, bricks broken, timbers'charred and rotten,
And the smell of the ghost of a house; these are ill-forgotton.

Gardens too, I hate; for I have seen gardens going
Into green slime and brown swamp, no flowers growing
In pits where old rains linger, stale snows harden,
And only graves, where roses grew, still tell of the garden.

And I hate plowed lands, who have been set a-plowing
Crooked furrows to fight in, where the guns go sowing
Bodies of men in the trenches, and grey mud covers
Fools, philosophers, failures, labourers, lovers.

Quenched now, flame into smoke, in the brightness and boldness
Of the men were my friends in their life, turned staleness and
    coldness;
Indestructible old things, be you now my friends,
Take me into the old life as the new life ends.

I have gone up to the dark wood where the old things grow.
The badger and the snail and the sloe.
I will dwell in the ground there and learn there to cherish
The old things for the new things, the loved things, perish.

I have gone to the woods where in ages before me
Grappling, my hairy ancestors got me and bore me;
I have sought out the caves where, pursued, my mothers
Whimpered, and turned to receive their grunting lovers.

Yet not in their time love peace nor knew it,
Who, scented afar their quarry, grew stiff to pursue it,
When a brown arm, shot from the bough, caught the bird for
    plunder,
Or limb on the ground tore the screaming rabbit asunder.

So no peace shall I find, in all the ages,
Short and harsh man's life is and death is its wages.
Life goes hot from the throat, by the cry made holy,
Or passes, bedded in towns, with unction, slowly.

Here, day follows on day, but, among their number
Hidden, a day shall dawn when alert from slumber
I no more shall arise; but these limbs lie rotten,
Cold in the cave, by insects forgotton.
None to bury me, none to remember me, none to pity
Swift shaking leaves from my sides, I fly to the city,
There find friends in my need who will not forsake me;
Thence in fullness of days my deathe shall take me

First Five Stanzas written: 1917
The Rest written: November 1918
Published in the New Statesman, 30th November 1919

Aviator Ignotus

Fine boys; clear-eyed, cool-headed, iron-nerved,
With golden confidence their faces shine.
Not fearless, careless p'raps; you had observed,
When theirs were cradeled, bibbed, that air in mine.
My risks were never theirs, a rivalry
Not hostile – my achievement slight appears; –
To instruct man's inexperience to fly!
There is no mercy in time for pioneers.
But the whole world was then my flying-ground;
I dared the Atlantic; and the Alps obeyed
My discipline. Myself no routine bound
As binds these boys to-day the code I've made.
War came: I might have sped North, East, West, South,
Scattering death, an Ace to conjure by
Both sides the line, my name in every mouth . . .
I was matured, or staled. I do not fly.
. . . Experience kept me placed. Hope shewed a way
Through difficulties. Now to overcome
A thousand flaws of structure. Every day
Power increased. Mastery – and what subjects. Some
You see to-day here, veterans now. The most
Have outflown life – died to expose a fault
Survivors may correct. Counting the cost
Were mawkish. Progress sweeps us. Who cries, "Halt!"
When each day dawns more gloriously on each
Young face by dawn's experience gilded? How
Grasp yesterda's ideal in this day's reach,
Point the way clear whence we fall, grasping, now?
Theirs the flights, failures, victories, rewards,
The Phaethon ardour and the Icarus lapse.
They scour the heavens: I pace the office boards;
They scan the earth's wrinkles; I adjust the maps.

Their life, death theirs; yet mine the risk they run.
I shape their wings – I shake them forth in the air
Emancipate, radiant as the sun.
Dazzle my eyes? My brain still guides them there.
So mine an unfamed glory: mine remorse
For ruin care had p'haps averted. Mine
The lamplit vigilance, directs their course;
The undulant order of their battle line.
. . . So I shall serve my time out and retire.
"A peace-time fighter – dug-out – does no stunts;
Commander, British Empire – under fire
From Zepps – not when he Cook'stoured round the fronts."
My epitaph . . . When flight was deemed absurd
I flew, unarmed, clean-handed, risked your mirth.
I, not these boys, am kinsman to the bird:
May have me, body and bones, but in the air
Let my ghost loiter, careless and content.
My hand has loosed no meteor-torment there.
I'll haunt there, as I flew there, innocent.
My worth rests somewhere in the base of things,
Solid, but, young upspringing straight alive . . .
Enviable, eh? That curled one, now, the King's
Just spoken to – I taught him his nose-dive.

*Outside Buckingham Palace, May 1918. Published in the Westminster
Gazette. Told Charles Prentice 8.12.22 that Wilfred Owen liked it.*

The Willow Tree Bough

My heart's at the war with a good natured rifleman,
Where he stands firing the foreman to slay,
While he was home with us laughter and liveliness,
Night time or church time twas all holiday.

Friends who fall in with a good natured rifleman,
Tell him his Helen abides by her vow,
Just as she swore when her William last January
Carv'd his sweet name on the willow tree bough.

He's got moustaches, a good natured rifleman,
Curl'd at each end like the fiery young moon.
Yes and he marches so deft and delightfully,
All the old streets here still echo the tune.

Now that he's given himself up for a soldier,
All over the world his brave body to show,
How can you wonder that I in my anxiousness
Weep with my eyes on the willow tree bough?

Here's to their health the greenjacketed gentlemen,
Scouring their enemies over the plain,
Fighting like seals in a lickerish estuary,
Soon may old Winchester see them again.

Soon may the children are yet to be born to me,
Standing around like young shoots in a row.
Hark to the eldest one, spelling so easily
Worm-eaten words Ah! On the willow tree bough.

Dated: 30th October 1918
Later set to music by Edward J Dent

Summer Thunder

In the stale afternoon he dragged unwilling
Feet through the sweltering fields, and crossed the stile,
And presently lay exhausted on the hillside,
And stretched out beneath him, mile on mile,
Parched watermeads, with cattle hardly moving ,
And at the valley's end a brooding pile;
The grey cathedral standing before the horizon,
Whose bells, rung drowsily, seemed even there to fill
The heavy air with continuous murmur;
Then ceased; and all was silence. Hot and still
The air dropped over him like a thick cloak, stifling;
Wearily he turned his face towards the hill,
And knew, he was come into the King's Palace,
And timidly walked through corridors, down flights
Of echoing iron stairs that never ended;
And moved, pressed hurrying on, through days and nights.
And sometimes paused at spider-haunted windows
To catch the blinding flare of beacon lights,
And heard artillery grumble in the distance,
For he knew that they warred against that Palace, when
He saw the gnomes come chattering from their chambers,
Well-armed for battle; little, dusky men
Complaining, shrill, in the old early language,
Conscious that Fate was falling upon them then,
Suddenly, in the midst of the field of baffle,
He stood bewildered, with a roar in his hears
As the two armies frantically crashed together.
Men running forward and falling. Groans and cheers,
And the sobbing breath of quiet men keenly fighting
Around him; then he was aware of the shower of spears
That pierced his hands and his head and his whole body,
Till he lay helpless, a captive, upon the ground,

Shattered and spilt like a bowl that is fallen and broken,
All his limbs melted into one aching wound,
Trodden under the grass . . . the line of battle
Surged over him and away, till the pitiless sound
Was soothed into silence. Then in a burst of sunshine,
Out of a rainbowed sky a huge voice spoke
Far off, and ceased, and he knew in that clear moment
That fate had made an end of the mountain-folk;
He felt their echoing Palace filled with quiet,
The grass wave over it; then saw, as he awoke,
All over his body large raindrops fall drilling.

Published 1922 in the London Mercury

LOVE AND DEDICATORY POEMS

Untitled Poem

You bid me go, but there is nothing shewn
In your controlled tone
No; not that quiet sound
Can deal me any deadly wound
Even if you're as cold yet I am firm as stone

And still unmoved I feel you clasp my hand
Your touch I can withstand
For still the spark of pride
Within me has not wholly died
By the remembered breath of early feeling fanned

Then as you hold my hand and speak my name
A sudden withering of flame
Sharper than lightning flies
From that live furnace in your eyes
And dissolute I melt in overwhelming shame

Written in pencil (at university, by handwriting) on back of family tree
(in thin ink).

The Beechwood

Tired we are of people and the roaring town-
While on every beech bough hot buds burst and grow
To a tender wonder of greenness: we will go
Now into the greenwoods and there lie lightly down,
Lie down and watch the sun fluttering through green leaves;
I will lie still and just gaze on you were you lie,
And you will smile to see the delicate new sky
Pierce those new silken curtains that the green beech weaves.
Happy, happy dreamers! But, before evening; -
While gently, like the spirit of some slain young thing
A white moon creeps up where little clouds go racing;-
We will rise and shake off last years brown leaves that cling,
And cross the valley slowly, slowly climb the hill
Then laugh to hear our respectable streets so still.

Written: Macvitties 5th Feb 1910

Untitled

"Since my life makes your virtue tremble and blush," he said;
"It will never hurt you to hear that I am dead."

"Since you give me sorrow, an empty heart and sore;
"I sail," he said, "Tomorrow for the high plains of war."

"Wise hills stand behind it, gentle streams go through
Broad vallies. May I find it friendlier than you."

"When the war is ended, you will come back to me
With your sore heart mended and your head by my knee."

"Perhaps;" he answered, turning. "Death here, life's there to choose."
He's gone. Still my dead burning eyes grope and beg for news.

News of dark men firing through mist sheets on thin downs,
News of bright girls a-hiring in the streets of their towns-

Peace now! The day is over;
Small lights on the far shore flame up fail and recover.
No voice, nor any oar sounds and I have no lover.

Written: Macvitties – 4th July, 1911

Sonnet

Thinking Love's Empire lay along that way
    Where the new-duggen grave of friendship gaped,
We fell therein, and, weary, slept till day.
    But with the sun you rose, and clean escaped,
Strode honourably homeward. Slowly I
    Crept out upon the crumbling otherside,
And thither held my course where Love should lie
    But thorn-set hedges rent my Cloke of Pride,
And stones my feet, that yet no nearer came.
    I gazed for you but you were gone from sight
To Honour in an honest house of shame.
    Should I press on – hills hide the road, and night.
        But if I turn – the bitter pathway lies
        Across that hole where, smothered, Friendship
        dies.

Published in The New Witness, June 7, 1918
Meant for Wilfred Owen
Originally Written as "My Mistake" in April 1909

All Clear

Last night into the night I saw thee go,
    And turned away; and heavy of heart I clambered
Up the steep causeway: weary, late and slow
    By my lone bed arrived. But, I enchambered,
Out cried the sullen alert artillery:
    Shrilled watchmen: woke the slumbering streets in riot.
And, was I sad for my night's swallowing thee,
    Then I was glad because thy night was quiet.
For, we'rt thou near, I should not be afraid,
    But, thou away, there is no harm to fear;
Thou not endangered, I am undismayed,
    Yet hence must danger hide when thou art here.
So I am doubly saved and safe shall stay
    Thine arms being close or all thyself away.

Published in The New Witness September 27, 1918
Meant for Wilfred Owen

Three poems to friends published as the dedications in the *Song of Roland*

To W.E.S.O.

When in the centuries of time to come,
Men shall be happy and rehearse thy fame,
Shall I be spoken of then, or they grow dumb,
Recall these numbers and forget this name?
Part of thy praise, shall my dull verses live
In thee, themselves- as life without thee – vain?
So should I halt, oblivion's fugitive,
Turn, stand, smile know myself a man again.
I care not: not the glorious boasts of men
Could wake my pride, were I in Heaven with thee;
Nor any breath of envy touch me, when,
Swept from the embrace of mortal memory
Beyond the stars' light, in the eternal day,
Our contented ghosts stay together.

Written December 1918
To Wilfred Owen after his death

To Philip Bainbrigge

Philip, here, at the end of a year that, ending,
Spares for mankind a world that has not spared thee;
O'er the sole fathom of earth that may know thee, bending
Dry-eyed, bitterly smiling, I now regard thee.
Friend – nay, friend were a name too common, rather
Mind of my intimate mind, I may claim thee lover:
Thoughts of thy mind blown fresh from the void I gather;
Half of my limbs, head, heart in thy grave I cover:
I who, the solder first, had at first designed thee
Heir, no health, strength, life itself would I give thee.
More than all that has journeyed hither to find thee,
Half a life from the wreckage saved to survive thee.

    *   *   *   *   *

Fare thee well then hence; for the scrutinous Devil
Finds no gain in the faults of thy past behaviour,
Seeing good flower everywhere forth from evil'
Christ be at once thy Judge, who is still thy Saviour,

Who too suffered death for thy soul's possession;
Pardoned then thine offences, nor weighed the merit:
God the Father, hearing His intercession,
Calls thee home to Him. God the Holy Spirit

Grant thee rest therefore: a quiet crossing
From here to the further side, and a safe landing
There, no shore-waves breaking nor breeze tossing,
In the Peace of God, which passeth our understanding.

Christmas 1918

To Ian MacKay

Like fire I saw thee
Smiling, running, leaping, glancing and consuming;
Like fire thine ardent body moving;
Scorching and scouring the mind's waste places
Like fire: like fire extinguished.

Now in my hands
Holding thy book, these ashes of thee;
Still fire I know thee
Gloriously somewhere burning,
Who wast so keen, more keenly;
Who wast so pure, more purely;
Beyond my vision,
Somewhere before God's Face,
Eternal.

October 1919

Dedication In Beowulf

To Richard Reynolds Ball

What! My loved companion, / in coldness liest thou,
Finished with life, / in a land afar?
From friends divided, / to death forsaken,
Farest thou alone / on Fate's errand,
The way of the world when / by the Will of God
Goeth to him again / the gift He hath given,
His loan of life. / No less I mourn thee
Than did I those / whom Death went thieving,
Willing youths / in the years of war,
Our friends and our fellows, / though fain was I of them
When keenly I bewailed / my battle-comrades,
Finding them murdered / upon many fields.
When a little knave I was / knew I thee first
Since before me thou / wast born among men,
An elder friend / to those following after.
For thou wast living / thirty years long,
Summers and winters, / and four years following
Busily kept me / among killing banes.
Then thou wast with foreign races, / Russ-men and Frenchmen,
Serbs and Poles, / in the passing seasons,
Six winter-tides, / while the tale of war
Pressed to an end: / peace came after,
Prosperity promised / to the peoples on earth,
Welfare after warfare. / Would they then readily
Wind away, / the warriors mostly,
A straggling few / of the fierce strugglers
Who out of the battle / had borne them alive.
But thou wast for returning / whither trouble waited,
Famine and fever / among friendless folk.
Nor was it any time then till / must taste thou also

The dreary cup / that Christ erst drank,
Sad in soul, / the Sinners' Shepherd,
The holy Lord, / whose heart ever loveth us,
The Son of God / in the Garden of Sorrows,
On the eve of Death. / Even so didst thou also,
By ever fated. / Freely everywhere wentest thou,
Shooting not at enemies, / armed with no shield
Against threats / of evil-thinkers,
But smiling at terrors, / true and simple.
Diedest thou as thou hadst lived, / dutifully.
Nor have I heard of a man / having more of happiness,
Stronger and kinder / to kinsmen and strangers,
A warden of the wretched. / Will they easily
Bear in mind, / who may hereafter be born,
The English friend / of their fathers of old,
Who helped them in need, / and held back nothing,
Gave his life / for the love of God.
They will say that of men / in mind and soul
In mood the mildest, / in mercy and pity
Best beloved, / most beautiful to remember
In the days / of this our life.

June 1920

University in Time of Peace

Most learned Masters, are ye of one mind
These solemn days of Peace to celebrate
In glad oblivion, and to reintegrate
Our broken Enemy, calling him kin and kind?
So be it: much in his doctrine can ye find
Of iron strength, that may sustain our State
When Pillage, Arson, Massacre congregate
Under her flag, and Famine scowls behind.

Nay, England: now that thine old warfare ends,
Unlearn Hell's lessons, forfeit the fool's trust
Thou hast in them; and make elsewhere amends.
Let the Curtane Sword, which proclaims thee Just
Among the Nations, redden and melt with rust
More honourably than in the blood of friends.

Dated October 1920

Translator's Dedication-Swann's Way – Part I

To E.J.C (Eva Cooper)

Here, Summer lingering, loiter I
    When I, with Summer, should be gone . . .
Where only London lights the sky
    I go, and with me journeys "Swann"

Whose pages' dull, laborious woof
    Covers a warp of working-times,
Of firelit nights beneath your roof
    And sunlit days beneath your limes,

While, both at once or each in turn,
    Sharp-tongued but smooth, like buttered knives,
We pared, with studied unconcern,
    The problems of our private lives;

Those tiny problems, dense yet clear,
    Like ivory balls by Chinese craft
Pierced (where each hole absorbed a tear)
    And rounded (where the assembly laughed).

Did all our laughter muffle pain,
    Our candour stimulate pretence?
Fear not. I shall not come again
    To tease you with indifference.

Yet I may gaze for Oakham spire
*   Where London suns set, watery-pale,*
And dream, while tides of crimson fire
*   Sweep, smoking, over Catmos vale.*

C.K.S.M
Michaelmas 1921

Translator's Dedication – Within a Budding Grove Part I

To K.S.S (Katherine Shaw Stewart)

That men in armour may be born
        With serpent's teeth the field is sown;
Rains mould, winds bend, suns gild the corn
        Too quickly ripe, too early mown.

I scan the quivering heads, behold
        The features, catch the whispered breath
Of friends long garnered in the cold
        Unopening granaries of death,

Whose names in solemn cadence ring
        Across my slow oblivious page.
Their friendship was a finer thing
        Than fame, or wealth, or honoured age,

And – while you live and I – shall last
        Its tale of seasons with us yet
Who cherish, in the undying past,
        The men we can never forget.

Bad Kissingen
C.K.S.M
July 31, 1923.

Translator's Dedication – The Guermantes Way

To
Mrs H—,
On her Birthday

OBERON, *in the* ATHENIAN *glade,*
Reduced by deft TITANIA'S *power*
Invented arts for NATURE'S *aid*
And from a snowflake shaped a flower:
NATURE, *to outdo him, wrought of human clay*
A fairy blossom, which we acclaim to-day.

HEBE, *to high* OLYMPUS *borne,*
Undoomed to death, by age uncurst,
XERES *and* PORTO, *night and morn,*
Let flow, to appease celestial thirst:
Ev'n so, untouched by years that envious pass
YOUTH *greets the guests to-night and fills the glass.*

HESIONE, *for a monstrous feast,*
Against a rock was chained to die;
Young HERCLES *came, he slew the beast,*
Nor won the award of chivalry:
E.S.P.H., *whom monsters hold in awe,*
Shield thee from injury, and enforce the law!

Acrostic poem spelling Oriana Huxley Haynes.

SATIRICAL VERSE

The Child's Guide to an Understanding of the British Constitution.

Third Lesson

There are no stars in all the sky
Outshine the blest Dioscuri;
Castor and Pollux, sons of Zeus
Immortal, and by common use –
     Called patrons of seafaring men,
     Who lamp their radiance back again.

As none in heaven can match their worth
So is it with two men here on earth;
Still with two great brethren we implore
To guide our helm in peace or war:
     For there is none alive whose bread is
     More buttered than the brothers Geddes.

Not very long ago they came
To wealth, emolument and fame;
While the sea rolls o'er British ships,
And all our sun is in eclipse,
     And England hardly seems alive,
     Quite suddenly the pair arrive.

Five years since, men who know aver,
One was a Railway Manager
The other an Anatomist,
Till in a trice, ere any wist,
     They outstripped all their fighting pals
     As generals or admirals.

"Or" say I, for alternately
They've governed us by land and sea,
And ever dressed themselves anew
In khaki and in navy blue,
      Enrolled recruits – laid railway tracks.
      (Meanwhile their sister ran the Waacs.)

Now Whitehall, very sore afraid,
Sees Auckland at the Board of Trade;
Where, while he guards his secret box
Canals, roads, rivers, railways, docks,
      Tubes, omnibuses, charabancs,
      Eric accepts with grateful thanks.

But there are other stars as well
Of which I have no time to tell;
The Harmsworths, likewise sons of Heaven,
In a number are not two, but seven;
      A Pleiad constellation form
      And keep each other bright and warm.

Also two Samuels there are
But one of them's a fallen star;
A vast contractual obligation
Divides his loyalty with the nation:
      So now in Warsaw he renews
      The ties that bind us to our Jews.

Published in *The New Witness September 5 1919*

The Child's Guide to an Understanding of the British Constitution.

Fourth Lesson

"Say, whose is that enormous jaw?
So grim a man I never saw.
His body glows with latent heat:
He seems some General in retreat,
Or else some Calvanistic Parson."

"My child, that is Sir Edward Carson."

"What is his function in the State?"

"I think, 'tis just to irritate;
Like the torpedo-fish, he stings
For joy at hurting helpless things.
He loves to hear the Irish groan,
A people he has made his own."

Published in The New Witness September 12, 1919

The Child's Guide to an Understanding of the British Constitution.

Fifth Lesson

"EX AFRICA SEMPER—"

When to Deauville the Premier retires, for economy,
And the War-Lord kills grouse with his usual bonhomie,
And the Highbury Chancellor utters no sound,
Lord Beaverbook lies, with his ear to the ground.

There are cards on French tables, and horses that run,
There are birds at Dunrobin that rise to the gun;
The dispatch-box stands empty, and silent the phone,
But Lord Beaverbrook dreams in a world of his own.

What ails him? He listens with evident pain,
As rumour runs swift through the shades of Shoe Lane;
Our army grows restive, depressed is our trade,
And Lord Beaverbrook numbers the men he has made.

The suggestion is offered, he knows not by whom,
To exalt Mr Churchill in Chamberlain's room;
In a spending Department his presence spells risk,
But he may prove less costly in charge of the Fisc.

In Treasury Chambers they look with demur
On a change that is terribly apt to occur;
But Lord Beaverbook vows, 'twixt a curse and a sob,
That Colonel Grant Morden's the man for that job.

Though no Dope he's provided, he'll furnish us yet
With the means to extinguish our National Debt,
By bartering England for sixpenny shares;
Then Beaverbrook's Lord will have answered his prayers.

*   *   *   *   *

An African warrior, bulky and black,
From the hosts of Archangel comes suddenly back,
A man of experience rare among men:
And Lord Beaverbrook harvests the fruit of his pen.

What the Nation and Statesman discovered last year
Is most wonderful news to this ardent young Peer;
In so massive a witness, returned from the Front,
Lord Beaverbrook feels there is scope for a stunt.
With trenchant invective, the man from the spot
Denounces the strategy, writes up the plot,
With a medley of politics, half-understood;
Lord Beaverbrook reads it and sees it is good.

The Herald is touched by his chivalrous air,
But an ominous silence fills Printing House Square;
And in Aldwych the outlook continues the same
Till they've got to the bottom of Beaverbrook's game.

Well he's "served with distinction," and earned his rewards,
A place in the Commons, a robe in the Lords,
An Usher's appointment at the back of the Throne,
Where Lord Beaverbrook governs, by laws of his own.

Historians of England, remember the day
When out of Shoe Lane, in their battle array,
Like the death-dealing crest of a cataract, poured
Little Jeff with his coronet, Mutt with his sword.

Published in The New Witness: September 19, 1919

Latitudes and Longitudes

You distress me, Mr Bullitt;
When I shew a leg, you pull it,
And you make me shew my hand,
Which is more than I can stand.

I was lost in dreams immense,
Georgics in the Future Tense.
You recall my past and present,
Bullitt, and it isn't pleasant.

It is clear that you and I are
One a dupe and one a liar;
If the fault be proved in me,
Bullitt, where will England be?

Bullitt, had I guessed that you were
Just a Yankee interviewer,
Both your ears a-cock for tips;
I'd have locked, not licked my lips.

This is no mere mask of virtue,
Bullitt; I am truly hurt. You
Know my secret; don't declare it,
Bullitt, for I could not bear it.

II.
Woodrow Wilson, how could men in
Our position treat with Lenin?
And, still more preposterous,
How could Lenin treat with us?

Lenin I believe to be
Much the same as you or me;
But, had Winston Churchill heard,
Shouldn't I have got the bird?

Men who say things quite untrue essay
To work my downfall through the U.S.A.:
Haven't I enough to face,
Wilson, in my native place?

Patronage, I understand,
Flows like water from your hand;
Whosoever else may fill it,
Don't let Bullitt find a billet.

Published in The New Witness, September 26, 1919

The Challenge

Red: KKt to KR6 White: KRP x P

From the red a nimble knight*
Overleaped the pawns, to fight
For his King, lest any check there should surprise him;
From the white a stalwart rook
Cried his challenge:—" If that Duke
Didn't move back into safety, he'ld chastise him."

Said the Duke, "I keep my health
By the use I make of wealth,
And I act as any sober man who could, would."
"What about the wretched lives,"
Smillie asked, "of miners' wives,
While yours is feasting Royalty at Goodwood?"

And some say the Duke won,
And some say that Smillie won,
And some say the palm has gone to neither;
But this one thing I've found:
All the coal is under ground,
And till some one goes and gets it, it will lie there.

Then that little ginger Duke
Said, "You're nothing but a crook
Who would flout a peer of George the Third's creation.
Since it seems, your only mission
Is to propagate sedition,
You had better leave the counsels of the Nation!"

Smillie heard him snort defiance
At the workers' Triple Alliance,
And replied, "I see no reason yet for panic;
But I'll cheerfully resign
Any office that is mine,
If you'll relinquish Albury and Alnwick.

So the "Post" thinks the Duke won,
The "Herald" thinks that Smillie won,
The "Spectator" thinks itself is winning, hands down.
And the "Nation" is inclined
(If it hasn't changed its mind)
For an All-Young-England Party, under Lansdowne.

*For this charming image I am indebted to Mr E.T. Raymond
and the "Outlook"

Published in The New Witness October 3rd, 1919

The Child's Guide To An Understanding Of The British Constitution.

Sixth Lesson

"This is indeed a pleasure rare!
    I see that the Ministry complete.
But, oh! What means that empty chair?"
    "My child, that is the Premier's seat,
And he is hardly ever there."

"I've heard of him, and often meant
    Ask how he reached that high position."
"By years of loyal discontent,
    And sometimes threatening sedition
He won his way to Government."

"When grave industrial unrest
    Removed him from the Board of Trade,
They set him o'er the Treasure Chest;
    Though at accounting, I'm afraid
He was not always quite his best.

"Amid the Nation's wealth he'd sit
    Penniless; till, by evil chance,
A friend advised: so, bit by bit,
    He found an interest in Finance;
And Mr Isaacs fostered it.

"But then he did not stand alone;
    Others, who also feared exposure,
When the debate grew warm in tone
    Would resolutely move the closure.
Still, by degrees, the truth was known.

      *   *   *   *   *

"After some weeks of penitence
    By Beauchamp's side he took his stand
And used his utmost eloquence
    To frighten farmers off the land.
They did not trust his evidence.

      *   *   *   *   *

"The war, whose varying circumstance
    Gave some a gilded coronet
And many an unknown grave in France,
    For him had something nobler yet;
He saw, and quickly seized his chance.
"For in his country's keen distress,
    He found occasion to attack
His elder colleagues supiness;
    While those that would have held him back
Could not get near him for the Press.

"So, as by magic, he achieved
    His secret, ever-cherished ends
But found in those whom he belived
    Not patrons only but true friends,
He had been cruelly deceived."

"What can a man so mighty fear?"
    "He guides his bark o'er perilous seas:
On either side of him appear
    Converging vast Symplegades,
Lord Northcliffe and Lord Rothermere.

"He trims his sail; attempts to glide
    Between; pauses, and looks again;
The towering cliffs on every side
    Are white with bones of better men.
He wishes now he had not tried.

"To drop his pilot in mid-ocean,
>Had stopped his ears to Billing's case;
Though, at the time,, he had no notion
>'Twould smirch so many with disgrace.
For now he rather dreads commotion.

*   *   *   *   *

"He cannot always trim those sails;
>The future we may now divine:—
When, finally, his spirit fails,
>He'll take his pension and resign;
And then, each Sabbath morn, in Wales,

"With fiery rhetoric, fast and faster,
>Parsons and Squires once more abuse,
Predict the Establishment's disaster—
>But there's one text he'll never use;
'Had Zimri peace, who slew his master?'"

Published in The New Witness, October 10th, 1919

The Child's Guide -To An Understanding Of The British Constitution.

The Cecils.

When the Sixth Edward pined upon his throne;
And Mary nursed her miseries alone;
And wearied England once again drew breath
In the large splendour of Elizabeth,
One morning in a burst of sultry flame,
The Church of England and the Cecils came;
And Englishmen must suffer, will or nill,
The Church of England and the Cecils still.

If one election in a crowded hour,
Should bring six hundred Cecils into power
With sixty-nine more, each come close relation;
'Twould leave Lloyd George in hopeless isolation.
Lloyd George, whom no such prospects e'er defeats,
Adds to the Commons thirty-seven seats;
Wherefore the Cecils too must add three dozens
To their established hierarchy of cousins.

Published in The New Witness
October 17th 1919

The Child's Guide -To An Understanding Of The British Constitution.

Seventh Lesson.

'Who are they, Father, say again,
That little band of noblemen
From whom the others stand aloof,
As if they feared some grave reproof?
  They must be very, very great!"
  "My child, that is the Fourth Estate.

"First is the Master-Journalist,
The Sovereign Rationalist
Who word the people's faith dispels
In other statesmen's miracles;
  He can do all things, save replace
  The men he smothers in disgrace.

"His brother's next, Lord Rothermere,
The sluggard's Sunday pulpiteer
Whom he that lies abed may read
Expounding all the plain man's creed.
  Each Monday morning down he climbs
  And holds his Mirror to the Times

"And who is yon distinguished chief
That sports the blushing maple-leaf,
With th'air of some anointed King?
That, surely, is the real thing!"
  "Hush: no respectful child should look
  Upon the Baron Beaverbrook

"He is the power behind the throne;
He works in secret and alone.
While most generously he purveys
Those most amusing Picture-Plays,
        He rule, with telephone and pen,
        The lives of even littler men."

"And that Lord Bathurst, what is he?"
"A man of fairish family
Who, growing old, and rather stout,
With nothing much to think about,
        Respects the noblest names alone:
        The Hapsburgs', and, of course, his own.
"But every one is not a crook
Of Bathurst, Burnham, Beaverbrook,
Cadbury, Northcliffe, Rothermere;
So everyone is not a Peer.
There are some commoners as well,
        Notably Hulton and Dalziel.

"The sporting Muse of Hulton sings
Whene'er his horses race the King's;
Dalziel, last year, saw what he thought
Must be the truth in print, and bought
        The sheet whose fearless columns told it:
        But truth remained with them that sold it."

"Father, it is not clear to me
Whence these derive authority.
For, I was led to understand,
Kings, Lords and Commons rule this land."
        "True in a sense, but none the less,
        They get their orders from the Press."

Published in The New Witness: October 24th 1919

Fountains Of Honour.

A Hymn For The New Year.

Sing *Noel, Noel, Noel, Noel!*
The Tubes have been acquired by Joel;
And Albert Stanley's made a Peer
To bring us all a bright New Year,
Wheresoe'er we may be found
In omnibus or underground.

O Sapientia! The Board
Have ordered . . . . . . though they can't afford
Without depriving poorer friends
Of long-expected dividends . . .
An hundred thousand polished cars
With ermine straps on golden bars.

There, upon seats of crimson plush,
They hope to mitigate the crush;
Panels of stain-wood divide
The passengers on either side;
And in the midst of each, is set
Sir Albert's blameless Coronet

Noel, sing! for even now
The Underground approaches Slough,
And Omnibuses, very soon
Will bear us daily to Loch Doon;
Where, on a moorland, bleak and vast,
The Housing Problem's solved at last.

O Caledonia, cold and grey,
Meet nursemaid of an N.P.A.
Noel, Noel, Noel, sing!
News of the World to thee I bring.
Thy beacons flame o'er hilss and valleys
For Lord Ænigma of the Galleys,
While Egypt's Sphinxes glare, aghast
To see their Riddell solved at last.

In those adventurous border-lands
How like a moss-trooper he stands;
How every inch a Lord he'll look
When Rothermere and Beaverbrook,
With a few simple heart-felt words,
Present him to the House of Lords.

So now, of course, you'll understand
Why England is a happy land;
And why a happy people we,
Governed, as well or ill may be,
By such an Aristocracy.

Published in The New Witness
January 9th 1920

A Servile Statesman

"Sir Phillip Sassoon is . . ." Daily Press, *passim*

Sir Phillip Sassoon is the Member for Hythe;
He is opulent, generous, swarthy and lithe,
Obsequious, modest, informed and jejune,
A man in a million's Sir Phillip Sassoon.

Benevolent angels announced at his birth
That Sir Phillip Sassoon should inherit the earth,
While omniscient journalists boldly declare
That Sir Phillip Sassoon in a Prince of the Air.

He resides on the coast, between channel and down,
But he also possesses a mansion in town,
And he cannot be bothered to travel by train,
So Sir Phillip Sassoon has an aeroplane.

The South Eastern and Chatham's infested with crowds,
But Sir Phillip Sassoon goes astride of the clouds;
With his feet on the clouds and his face to the moon,
The way of an eagle's the way for Sassoon.

The homes he inhabits are costly but chaste,
For Sir Phillip Sassoon is unerring in taste,
And the daughters of Mammon may wish they were dead
Once Sir Phillip Sassoon has decided to wed.

Sir Phillip Sassoon is so kind to the poor
That no suppliant ever, who knocks at his door,
Is sent empty away; in addition to which
Sir Phillip Sassoon is so sweet with the rich.

Sir Phillip Sassoon and his sires, it appears,
Have been settled in England for several years,
Where their friendly invasion impartially brings
To our Cabinets wisdom, and wealth to our Kings.

When war upon Europe came down like a plague
He run by the stirrup of General Haig;
From his sword he's managed a salver to forge,
And he stands in the lobby of Mister Lloyd George.

Mr Wilson asserts, and he's sure to be right,
That Sir Phillip Sassoon made America fight,
When a friend in the city informs me to-day
That Sir Phillip Sassoon will make Germany pay.

Sir Phillip was always a double event,
In Baghdad a Banker, a Yeoman of Kent:
But now in four parts he's appearing at once,
As a lackey, a landlord, diplomatist, dunce.

NOTE. – This song may be sung in public, without fee, to the
tune of "The Laird of Cockpen."

Published in The New Witness, May 21, 1920